THE DOCTOR WAS A SAILOR

Claire Vernon

CHIVERS LARGE PRINT
Bath, England

CURLEY LARGE PRINT
Hampton, New Hampshire

Library of Congress Cataloging-in-Publication Data
Vernon, Claire.
  The doctor was a sailor / Claire Vernon.
    p.   cm.
  ISBN 0–7927–1993–X.—ISBN 0–7927–1992–1 (pbk.)
  1. Man–woman relationships—Fiction.   2. Physicians—Fiction.
  3. Nurses—Fiction.   4. Large type books.   I. Title.
  [PR6072.E735D6   1994]   93–49840
  823′.914—dc20   CIP

British Library Cataloguing in Publication Data available

This Large Print edition is published by Chivers Press, England, and by
Curley Large Print, an imprint of Chivers North America, 1994.

Published by arrangement with the author's estate.

U.K. Hardcover ISBN 0 7451 2230 2
U.K. Softcover   ISBN 0 7451 2241 8
U.S. Hardcover ISBN 0 7927 1993 X
U.S. Softcover   ISBN 0 7927 1992 1

© Claire Vernon 1966

Printed in Great Britain

THE DOCTOR WAS A SAILOR

CHAPTER ONE

Sally Hampton hurried down to the cabin, her cheeks flushed, eyes drowsy. As she opened the door, she said breathlessly:

'I'm terribly sorry, Mrs Dunn. I fell asleep on the deck.'

There was a little silence in the cabin as the two occupants stared at the girl in the doorway.

Sally Hampton might have stepped out of the pages of any glossy magazine of the year, with her straight, blonde, shining hair that swung with every movement she made, widely-spaced brown eyes and small turned-up nose. She was twenty years old, and looked about sixteen. She had a shy laugh and now as she saw that her employer was not alone, she felt her cheeks burning.

'I beg your pardon. I didn't see...' she began.

The ship's doctor stood up, his red hair untidy, his eyes amused as he looked down at the short slender girl.

'I hope you didn't get too much sun,' he said, his voice a little chiding. 'You girls are daft sometimes.'

'I didn't mean to...' Sally began and stopped abruptly. Her cheeks were hot for, as usual Dr Chart had made her feel young

1

and unsophisticated.

She hardly knew him. Indeed, she had only spoken to him when he paid his regular visits to her employer.

He turned away to talk to Louella Dunn, his face concerned, his voice grave.

'I see absolutely no need for you to worry,' he said slowly. 'In fact, your only danger is, Mrs Dunn, if you dwell too much on it and allow fanciful fears to take control. This six months of complete rest will make you a new woman...'

Louella Dunn laughed. It was a beautiful sound, Sally thought, as she gazed at her employer. In the long days of the voyage out from England, she had learned to like Louella Dunn very much indeed. Louella was forty-six years old, Sally knew, but she looked at least ten years younger. Louella had been a model in her youth and always looked perfectly groomed. Her ash-blonde hair was swept up from her wide serene forehead, her dark eyes wistful, her full mouth often sad. But then, Sally asked herself, who would not be sad when they felt well and yet were confined to bed for six whole months!

'I certainly hope so,' Louella Dunn said.

'I'll see you tomorrow,' Dr Chart said with a smile and left the cabin, without glancing at Sally as he passed her.

Sally's duties were light. She had been

engaged by Mrs Dunn as a combined nurse-companion-ladies' maid and now she helped her to the bathroom and later brushed the long ash-blonde hair and settled her comfortably in bed. Louella spent the day on the couch, sometimes being wheeled on deck in the wheel-chair, but saying she hated curious eyes and inquisitive questions so preferred to stay in her cabin.

'We'll have plenty of sunshine on the Island, Sally,' she said when Sally told her what a lovely day it was. 'I feel such a fraud when people ask what's wrong with me and I don't know.'

'But there must be something wrong,' Sally said earnestly. 'I mean, the doctors wouldn't say six months in bed if you were...'

'Malingering?' Louella Dunn supplied the word with a wry smile. 'I assure you I'm not. I loathe this...' Her hand vaguely indicated the couch, wheel-chair and the small table with bottles and pill boxes by her side. 'I can't wait for the six months to be up...'

Now as Sally ordered the dinner that would be brought in on a tray, she felt a wave of sympathy for Louella. It was so exciting—this long voyage from England to Tahiti and Louella was missing so much.

Sally glanced worriedly at the small gold travelling clock. Her name had been put down for the first sitting and she didn't want to be late.

'Your mother...' Sally said tentatively. Somehow she hated leaving Mrs Dunn alone in her cabin if she could help it.

Louella Dunn smiled. 'She'll be along in a moment, Sally. I'll be all right.'

'Thanks...'

Sally hurried to her own cabin, four decks below, and hastily changed into an amber-coloured silk frock. Her hair only needed a quick brush. She was used to making-up fast. The three girls with whom she shared the cabin all ate at the second sitting so she was alone.

Down in the dining saloon, she sat at a table for five people and was the only young person at it. There were two elderly couples who shared similar interests and talked to her occasionally in rather patronising voices.

After dinner, Sally hurried back to Mrs Dunn. The evenings, Sally felt, must be long and boring for the invalid, so Sally usually sat with her, playing an involved game of Patience or just talking. Mrs Dunn was always telling Sally not to worry about her and to go and join the young people and have fun, but Sally refused.

'This is my job,' she would say stubbornly and Louella would give a little shrug and smile at her.

'You're a nice girl, Sally,' she said.

Now as Sally opened the door, she heard

Mrs Dunn's mother speaking.

'Absolutely ridiculous, Louella,' she was saying in her sharp voice and she swung round as Sally entered. 'There you are, at last,' she added crossly.

'Mother, please...' Louella Dunn chimed in. 'Sally has just had dinner. She must have rushed it...'

'It's her job to stay with you...' Mary Ester said, her voice acid.

Mrs Ester was a tall, painfully thin woman. Always on a diet and complaining about it. Her smoky-blue hair was done elaborately, her cheeks rouged, her mouth too deep a red for a woman of her age, Sally thought, and then felt ashamed of herself. She had learned a lot more about Mary Ester than the elderly woman knew or would have liked, but Louella had never hidden the truth about the tough, painfully poverty-stricken youth she had spent, the times her father was out of work and food was scarce. When Mrs Ester talked of 'her estate' and her 'ancestors', Sally found it pathetic. Mrs Ester was obviously determined to forget her past. Indeed, she would never admit to it. But Louella had told Sally enough to make Sally understand why money was so terribly important to Mrs Ester and why she judged everyone by the contents of his wallet.

'We'd better go, Gran ... grandmother...' a quiet demure voice said.

5

Sally smiled sympathetically as Beryl Dunn stood up. Mrs Dunn had only two children. Johnny, a shy delicate boy of ten years of age, who would have already eaten with the children, and now be in bed. And Beryl. Sally was most sorry for Beryl who was seventeen years old yet made to dress and look like a young girl.

There was something scared in Beryl's quick glance. Beryl was dressed in a white dress. Very much like a tennis frock with godets flowing out into a full skirt. It was a demure length. And Beryl wore white socks and black shoes. Her long silky black hair was hanging to her shoulders, her dark eyes downcast, long lashes brushing her magnolia-like skin. Her whole expression was one of demure submission. Sally could not understand why Beryl did not complain or contest her grandmother's arbitrary rule—nor why Beryl's mother let it continue. Sally's cheeks had often burned as she heard remarks passed among passengers as they watched Beryl walking demurely with her grandparents.

The door opened and George Ester stood there.

'Come on ... come on,' he said gruffly.

He was a big man with a huge body, inclined to obesity but he refused to diet. His thick mop of white hair was always too long but no matter how often his wife told him so, he refused to have it cut.

'It's my hair,' Sally had heard him say once. 'I like it this way. I don't tell you to get your hair cut, do I?' he had asked his wife.

Sally liked him—as much as she disliked his wife. He must have been nearly seventy but had an active curious mind and was able to mix with different age-groups, interested in everything. He loved his grandchildren and spoiled them when his wife was not around. He also smoked a pipe but this he did only when his wife was there. Sometimes Sally wondered if he did it on purpose, because he knew it annoyed Mrs Ester so much.

It was blessedly quiet after the Esters and Beryl had left the cabin. Louella had eaten her dinner and seemed sleepy. After a few games of patience, Louella yawned.

'I think I'll have an early night, Sally. Go off and enjoy yourself,' she said.

Sally looked at the elegant woman in her blue silk dressing-jacket, her hair smoothly braided, her skin devoid of make-up yet looking perfect.

'It's not nine o'clock,' Sally pointed out.

Louella Dunn laughed.

'Look, Sally, when I engaged you, it wasn't as my shadow.'

Sally's cheeks were hot. 'I know but ... golly, I think you must be awfully lonely sometimes.'

7

Louella's dark eyes were thoughtful. 'I am, Sally, but I shan't be much longer. When we get to the Island, my husband'll be there. It's a whole year since he came out—it's been a long year...'

'Was it then you began to feel ill?' Sally asked gently.

Louella clasped her hands under her head and nodded.

'I guess so. Having a husband around keeps you on your toes. I was bored and lonely and began to get bad headaches. I took pills for them and...' She shrugged. 'I began to have black-outs and no one could find out the reason for them.' She sighed. 'I felt fit, just bored to tears. Then my husband cabled that I should join him with the children and...' She shrugged again. 'Here I am. Tied to a couch for six wretched months. He's not going to like it...'

There was an unusual note in Louella's voice. A frightened note, Sally thought.

'He'll understand...' Sally said soothingly.

'Oh yes,' Louella Dunn said. 'But that's not the point. Vincent is very much alive, always entertaining or going out. Very ... what's the word? ... extrovert. What sort of companion will I be?' she asked, and then, as if regretting having said so much, Louella looked at Sally. 'You're an introvert, aren't you, Sally? You've made very few friends on

8

the ship. I hoped you'd have a good time...'

'Oh, I have. A lovely time,' Sally said very quickly. 'It's been just wonderful, Mrs Dunn. I ... I guess I do find it hard to make friends. You see, I lost my parents when I was a small child and lived with my grandparents. They were very quiet people and never went out. I couldn't take friends home from school so I couldn't visit them...'

Louella nodded. 'I see. Well, I hope on the Island you'll learn to make friends, Sally. It's a lonely life without any. Now, run along, there's a good girl. I'm going to read for half an hour and then lights out. 'Night.'

'Goodnight,' Sally said obediently.

Outside the closed cabin door she hesitated. She knew there was dancing that night and also a film but she was too late for the latter. She decided to go up on deck. It was too early to go to bed.

She climbed the stairs slowly. Was she an 'introvert', she wondered. She had always wanted friends but, as she had told Mrs Dunn, it had been too difficult.

She stepped outside into the warm night air and caught her breath with delight as she saw the wide silver pathway across the water.

The deck was deserted. She could hear strains of music from the lounge where the small orchestra was playing before going to the 'White Inn' to play for dancing, later.

Sally found herself a chair and sank into it, propping her feet on the deck rail. She closed her eyes, loving the gentle rolling of the big ship, the quiet warmth, the absolute bliss of her new life.

'Sleepy?' an amused voice asked.

Sally sat up with a startled jerk. It was Dr Chart. Towering above her, his red hair smooth, his eyes teasing.

'I ... I ...' Sally found herself stammering and hating her own stupidity.

'May I join you?' he asked and, without waiting for her permission, pulled up a chair and sat by her side. 'Smoke?' he asked, offering her his cigarette case.

'No thank you,' Sally said politely. 'I don't smoke.'

He grinned. It was a funny lop-sided sort of grin but it did strange things to Sally. It also made her wish he would grin again, for it changed his whole face. No longer did he look as if he was laughing *at* her, but rather as if he was laughing *with* her. There was a terrific difference, she thought.

'Sensible girl. Have you never smoked?' he asked.

'Never,' she confessed. Suddenly she wondered if that sounded smug. 'You see, I was brought up by my grandparents and they disapproved of...'

'So many things?' Dr Chart asked gently. 'Is that why you find it hard to make

10

friends?'

Sally blushed. Was it so obvious, she wondered anxiously.

'In a way,' she began. She tried to explain. 'You see, when my parents died, I was very young and my grandparents were very old and it was wonderfully good of them to take me in. I guess I was an awful nuisance at times because as a child, I was always ill. They were good and patient with me and I loved them, so you see, I really never did anything they disapproved of, because it would have hurt them, and made them feel that somewhere they had failed and had not brought me up properly...' She stopped speaking abruptly, acutely embarrassed. How bored he must be.

But Dr Chart didn't look it. He leaned towards her, his face intent.

'I see,' he said thoughtfully. 'I imagine it was hard to make friends under such circumstances.'

'Oh, it was...' Sally said earnestly. 'I had friends at school but you can't go to their houses if you can't ask them to your own, can you? I mean, that wouldn't be right, would it? I don't think my grandparents realized. They didn't mean to put restrictions on me but they hadn't much patience with teenagers. Except...' She gave a shy little laugh. 'With me. And then they were wonderful.'

'Tell me...' Dr Chart said. 'What made you take this job? You're so young...'

'I'm twenty,' Sally said quickly.

He gave his lop-sided grin again. 'And I'm thirty-one! Quite an oldie to you, I suppose.'

Sally was startled. 'Are you as old as that...?' she began and stopped quickly as he roared with laughter.

When he stopped, he apologized. 'I wasn't laughing at you, Sally, but the somewhat one-sided compliment it was. It's odd, isn't it, how when you're young you want to look older but as you grow older, you want to look younger. I'm halfway—I don't want to look too old but then a doctor doesn't want to look too young, either.'

'I think Mrs Dunn looks wonderfully young, don't you?' Sally asked.

Dr Chart nodded. 'She's a very beautiful and very unhappy woman...'

'Unhappy?' Sally was startled for a moment and then nodded. 'Yes, but she'll be all right when she's with her husband and as soon as this wretched six months rest is over.'

'Will she?' Dr Chart asked, his voice odd.

Sally stared at him, puzzled. Remembering little things about her employer. Moments of wistfulness. A desperate note in her voice.

'Is she really ill?' she asked.

The doctor looked startled. 'She's a very

12

sick woman—' he said. 'Emotionally. Perhaps when she gets to the Island things will settle down. How do you get on with the Esters?'

Sally hesitated. 'I like him very much but...'

Dr Chart gave his odd grin again. 'I know! Amazing how much the little word "but" can convey. We're getting side-tracked. You were going to tell me why you took this job.'

'It's a long story,' Sally said, hesitating a little.

Dr Chart relaxed, his feet on the rail by Sally's, his chair slightly sideways so that he could look at her.

'I've all the time in the world,' he said, 'so fire ahead.'

It was a long story but Sally told it all—right from when she was fifteen and her grandmother was ill.

'I left school as soon as I could and got a job doing accounts in a local shop in Surbiton. They were good to me, letting me slip home often to see how Gran was. Then when I was seventeen, she died and Grand-dad just went to bits. Anyhow, he grew weaker and weaker, could hardly walk alone and yet we managed and then...' Sally paused, half-closing her eyes, remembering the horror of that never-to-be-forgotten moment.

'I was hurrying home from work.

13

Grand-dad hadn't slept well the night before and I was worried. It was a cold evening and there must have been something slippery on the road. I remember hurrying, then skidding and as I fell on my back, I saw this car swinging round the corner straight at me...' She paused and shivered. 'I've never been so scared and then something hit me and I...' She gave a little shrug. 'That was all. I woke up in hospital. I'd had concussion and a sprained wrist and a badly grazed leg.'

'And your grandfather?' the red-headed man prompted gently.

Sally's face was expressive. 'I was frantic about him. You see, it took quite a while before I could think properly or remember anything and then, when I did remember him—I'd got a visitor. A complete stranger.' She gave a little smile. 'It was Mrs Dunn. She was the driver of the car and was most frightfully upset about it. She said she had thought she'd killed me ... I told her about Grand-dad and she was absolutely wonderful. Went round at once and got him into a super-duper Rest Home. He loves it. Plenty of old men to natter to and telly, of course.'

'And you?'

'Me? Oh, I got better. Mrs Dunn insisted on sending me to Penzance for a month's holiday and I had a wonderful time.' Sally smiled. 'She's a most generous person, you know, Dr Chart.'

'You like her very much?'

Sally nodded, her straight long hair swinging vigorously.

'I certainly do. She's always good-tempered and kind and...' She laughed. 'She's lovely to look at and so nice to know...' She laughed again. 'That sounds like a pop song...'

He laughed with her. 'I believe it was, once. And then?'

Sally drew a long deep breath. 'I got a job in Knightsbridge and had a bed-sitter in Earls Court. I used to visit Grand-dad at weekends and he seemed much happier than when he was left alone all day in our flat in Surbiton. You see, we hadn't much money,' Sally said simply. 'I didn't earn much for I wasn't properly qualified and Grand-dad had only his pension so it was always a battle. About three months later, I got a letter from Mrs Dunn, asking me if I'd help her out...'

Sally laughed suddenly and turned impulsively to the man by her side. 'That is so typically Mrs Dunn. She plans a wonderful holiday for me and then asks me to "help her out"!' Sally laughed again. 'I went to see her and found she had been ill and ordered to bed and that she had heard from her husband who wanted her to come out...'

15

'I've often wondered why she didn't come out with him in the first place,' the red-headed doctor said thoughtfully.

Sally gave him a quick glance and hesitated. Was it disloyal to Mrs Dunn to discuss her? Yet why not?

'I think his original visit was ... what's the word? Oh yes, tentative. A sort of ... of exploratory trip. Johnny, the little boy, had been sick and Mrs Dunn didn't want to leave him and ... and quite honestly, I don't think Mr Dunn wanted his family along with him at the time.'

'I'm wondering if he wants the whole family this time,' Dr Chart said drily.

Sally glanced at him again quickly. 'I ... I don't think he wanted the Esters.'

'I'm sure I wouldn't,' Dr Chart said with a laugh. 'In-laws should be kept at a discreet distance.'

'Are you married?' Sally asked.

The words seemed to explode out of her mouth. She was dismayed to hear them for she had no right to ask...

Dr Chart gave his odd grin. 'You can bet your life I'm not. None of that tender trap business for me,' he added.

Sally flushed. 'You don't approve of marriage?'

He chuckled. 'For other people, yes. For me, definitely no.'

Sally frowned. 'Is it because you're a

16

doctor?'

Bob Chart stretched his long legs and yawned lazily.

'In a way, yes. In a way, no. You see, I never wanted to be a doctor,' he said, with surprising frankness. 'Trouble was, it was taken for granted I would be one. Both my parents are doctors and my sister is also one. I wanted to be a sailor...'

Sally was looking at his face. The chin was square. He had a deep, rather bossy voice. He looked strong.

'Wasn't that rather weak of you?' she asked, and once again, felt herself colouring. What right had she to say such a thing?

But he was not offended. 'I think it was just plain lazy,' he said honestly. 'Don't get me wrong, Sally. I like being a doctor. It's just that ever since I was a child, I've had a crazy dream about sailing round the world.' He laughed, a deep happy sound. 'Well, I'm on my way to making the dream come true.'

'You are?' Sally said eagerly. How much nicer Dr Chart was than she had thought him, she was realizing. He had seemed so patronising. But the man by her side was a different person. Sincere and friendly.

Bob Chart nodded. 'I leave the ship at Sydney. There I'm meeting up with an old friend who emigrated to Australia several years ago. We plan to work together and build our own boat and then sail round the world. He's married but we'll not take his wife along.'

'Why ever not?'

Bob Chart laughed. 'It's going to be pretty primitive and no place for a woman.'

Oddly enough, that irritated her. 'Why not? Lots of girls sail on yachts round the world.'

'Do they?' He grinned at her. 'Or is it just for publicity? I'm always reading about the way they defect and walk ashore. I suppose they fall for the skipper and he hasn't time for them so they get mad...'

'You don't like women, do you?' Sally said abruptly. Her hand flew to her mouth with a childish gesture. 'I'm sorry,' she added.

Dr Chart was looking at her strangely. 'Don't apologise. It's not quite the truth. It isn't that I don't like women, it's that they scare me.'

Sally began to laugh. 'Scare you...'

He nodded solemnly. 'My parents married while they were students. Lots of my friends are married. Often it proved to be a big mistake. But they all fell. In fact, I'm almost the last bachelor.'

'And you're proud of it?'

He gave his lop-sided grin. 'You can bet your life I am. I have ambitious plans, Sally, and love would shatter them. That's why I keep out of the way of predatory girls...' He grinned at her. 'That's a compliment, Sally, you know.'

'A compliment?' she said, bewildered.

He stood up. 'Yes, think it out. I've spent more time alone with you this evening than I have done with any girl on board. See you tomorrow. Pleasant dreams.'

His hand lightly ruffled her hair and then he was gone, his footsteps sounding on the deck loudly.

Sally sat very still, staring blindly at the moon-splashed sea. How was it a compliment? She caught her breath. Had he meant that she was not predatory? What did the awful word mean, anyhow, she wondered?

Next day she asked Mrs Dunn.

'Predatory...' Louella Dunn repeated slowly. 'I think it means chasing someone, being ruthless. I'm not sure.'

Sally, brushing her employer's ash-blonde hair painstakingly, turned the words over in her mind. Chasing someone. Ruthless. Dr Chart had said it was a compliment. Did he mean that she was not the type of girl who chased men? Or had he meant something else? Could it mean that she was not the type of girl whom men chased?

'There's a big dance tonight,' Mrs Dunn was saying, 'Sally, and I want you to go.'

'Oh no—' Sally said quickly. 'I don't know anyone and...'

'You never will if you go on at this rate,'

Louella Dunn said sternly. 'I've spoken to Dr Chart about it. He quite agreed and said it was unhealthy for a pretty girl of your age to hide in her shell. He'll look after you...'

'But when did he say this...?' Sally gasped.

Louella Dunn smiled. 'This morning, before breakfast. You hadn't come on duty and I had a blinding headache so I sent for him. I'm worried about you, Sally.'

'Please don't be. I'm very happy,' Sally said quickly.

Louella Dunn smiled. 'I know but you've got to learn to mix. We'll be entertaining a lot on the Island and I'll need your help, Sally. That's why I want to get you launched here where there's no pressure...'

'Pressure...' Sally repeated.

Louella nodded. 'My husband is a perfectionist. He expects his womenfolk to be poised, sophisticated, charming, diplomatic and everything else. You're going to find it very hard...'

'But ... but I'm not one of his womenfolk,' Sally said.

Mrs Dunn laughed. 'You'll have to stand-in for me, Sally, I'm afraid. I'll do all I can from my wheel-chair but Vincent likes his guests to be "scrambled", as he calls it, circulated and introduced. He loathes it when they get into a corner and stick there, talking to the same person. You'll have to do that for me, Sally.'

Sally stared in dismay. 'I shan't know what to talk about.'

Mrs Dunn laughed. 'You'll learn. Just ask them where they come from—about their work—their families, and you won't need to talk.'

'But tonight ... I haven't anything to wear...'

Louella Dunn laughed. 'What about that pretty rose-pink lace frock I bought for you. Just the thing.'

'But I shan't know anyone...' Sally cried. 'It'll be awful and...'

'You know Bob Chart,' Mrs Dunn said. 'He told me you both had a long talk last night on deck. You like him?'

The abrupt question startled Sally and to her dismay, she felt her cheeks hot.

'I didn't, at first,' she said honestly. 'But last night, he was different.'

She wondered why Mrs Dunn was smiling.

'In what way?'

Sally thought for a moment. 'He was more friendly. I usually feel I amuse him because ... well, honestly, it's hard to explain but I usually get the impression that he's laughing at me.'

Louella Dunn's eyes twinkled. 'Now that's not positive thinking, Sally ... With every man, you must think that he finds you

21

attractive and desirable.'

'But I couldn't...' Sally gasped.

'But you must,' Louella Dunn told her with a smile. 'Sally, people will judge you by the way you assess yourself. If you see yourself as shy, naive, young—they'll see you like that. What you must realize is that you are a very pretty girl, your hair is lovely and, what is a big asset, naturally lovely. You have a good skin, happy, friendly eyes, a pleasant manner. In fact, you are extremely attractive but by your very shyness, you are your own worst enemy. You must forget the image built by your grandparents, of a quiet, modest, well-behaved young lady.'

Sally stared at her. 'But...'

Louella touched her hand lightly. 'Believe me, Sally, you are a very pretty girl. Bob Chart said so ... and he's a man not easy to please...'

'Dr Chart...' Sally gasped. 'But...' She took a long deep breath. Had Dr Chart also said she was her own worst enemy?

A bit scared of where the discussion was leading them, Sally changed the subject. 'Is your headache really better?' she asked.

Louella Dunn smiled. 'Much better, thanks. Now run along and sun-bathe for a while. I'm going to write some letters.' She added: 'Sally ... run along and enjoy yourself.'

Sally hesitated. 'I'm not good at saying

these things,' she told her employer shyly. 'But ... but thanks for everything.'

She hurried down to her cabin. Her companions were just dressing and chattering, all of them sleepy after late nights. They greeted Sally in a friendly manner but she noticed they stopped talking. Hastily she changed into a black swim suit and slipped on white shorts and top, giving herself a hasty glimpse of her reflection in the mirror.

'A very pretty girl.' 'Your hair naturally lovely.' 'Happy eyes.' 'Extremely attractive,' she repeated silently. The sentences churned in her mind. Had Dr Chart said them?

Up on the sun deck, she found a place to lie down, carefully rubbing her skin with lotion. The glorious heat beat down on her skin, relaxing her completely. She closed her eyes, the brightness making shining stars revolve madly behind her closed lids.

Had Dr Chart said she was pretty? Did he really find her attractive?

A warm glow of happiness filled her. It was a real boost to her ego, she told herself. She had met boys at school and at work, had been out with them, danced with them, liked them. Of course, she had been kissed by them, had evaded their octopus-like arms at times, but none of them mattered very much. She had always been a bit surprised because they liked her, a little at a loss to know what to talk about, even somewhat disappointed because despite the romantic songs of love, she had not experienced it at all.

But now...

Her eyes tightly shut, she could see the tall lean man. His red hair, usually rumpled as if he had ruffled it with his impatient hand, his nose which had a freckle on the tip.

That dance, tonight, she thought worriedly. Dr Chart had said he would look after her. What did that mean, she wondered. A duty dance and then he would vanish? He had told her that he did not want to be involved with any girl, that he wanted to walk alone, that he feared what Sinatra called the 'tender trap'.

And how did she feel, Sally asked herself, turning over to brown the front of her legs and shoulders. What was her dream? Dr Chart's was to sail his yacht round the world. What was hers?

Maybe to travel? Maybe. But she knew without putting it in words what her dream was.

Her own little home. Two, or perhaps four children. Her own husband who would love her no matter how silly she was...

Something splashed on her. The coldness of the water jerked her out of her dream. She blinked at the tall, red-headed man in a swimsuit.

'Dr Chart...' she said.

He lay down beside her and grinned. 'Hi. Isn't it time you dropped the doctor part and called me Bob? After all, I call you Sally.'

She stared at him. 'Shouldn't you be...' she began.

'Working?' He laughed. 'I have been and I shall be, again. But first I wanted to see you. Mrs Dunn told me where you were. You're coming tonight, aren't you?'

It was not a question but a statement. Sally hesitated. She was startled when he took her hand in his.

'Please do, Sally,' he said gently.

She stared at him. 'Why ... why, I'd love to, thanks ... Bob.'

He stood up, pulling her to her feet. 'Come and have a swim. I've got ten minutes and then must be off. Meet me tonight at nine o'clock in the Smoking Room, Sally. We'll have a drink...' He looked down at her. 'I suppose you don't drink,' he added.

Sally shivered. This was the Bob she did not like. The one who teased her.

'I do drink,' she said firmly. 'My grandparents merely...'

'Taught you to drink in moderation...' Bob supplied the words with a grin. 'Come on, slowcoach...'

They jumped into the cool water, still hand in hand, and began to swim...

Ten minutes later, he left her and she felt

forlorn. The noisy crowd around her seemed to leave her out of things.

She hurried down to her cabin and hastily washed and dressed in a straight white sheath frock before going back to Mrs Dunn's cabin.

Louella Dunn was still writing letters. She looked up with a quick smile.

'So Bob Chart found you?'

Sally flushed. 'Yes.'

'And you're going tonight?'

Again Sally said simply: 'Yes.'

Louella smiled. 'I'm glad.'

CHAPTER TWO

Sally dressed with extra care that night and walked into the Smoking Room as the hands of the clock showed that it was just nine o'clock.

Bob Chart was waiting for her. He was on his feet as she walked towards him. Sally felt self-conscious. The lace frock fitted like a silk glove but she wondered if pink was too young. Everyone seemed to be staring at her.

Bob settled her in her chair, ordered drinks for them both and smiled.

'Very pretty—' he said tersely, grinned and added: 'The frock, of course.'

Sally blushed and wished for the millionth

time that someone had invented a cure for blushing.

'Mrs Dunn gave it to me,' she said, handling the soft silky lace. She looked up suddenly at the man opposite her. 'She was wonderful. She insisted on buying me clothes for the trip. She said it was a kind of uniform and they are the prettiest things I've ever seen.'

'How long are you staying on the Island with them?'

Sally shrugged. 'That's left to me. Mrs Dunn said that when I want to go home, she'll pay my return fare. She wants me to help her until she can walk about, anyhow. Her husband entertains a lot and she says she'll need me then.' Again, Sally blushed. 'The trouble is that she's so kind to me that I'm never sure if she's inventing things to make me happy.'

'Don't you think that's rather far-fetched,' Bob Chart asked. 'I mean, why should she?'

'I think she was so upset about the car accident...'

'I think she likes you...'

Sally sighed. 'I just don't feel sometimes I'm earning my salary. It's much too high...'

'Stop worrying about things, Sally,' Bob said, his voice sharp. 'Louella Dunn needs someone like you as a friend, someone young with whom to laugh, someone she can make happy...'

'Why doesn't she make Beryl happy, then?' Sally asked abruptly, and then wished she hadn't.

'Beryl?' Bob's eyebrows lifted. 'She strikes me as a very happy normal girl of seventeen.'

'Oh, Bob, she isn't,' Sally said quickly. 'How can she be? I mean, those ridiculous clothes, like something out of another generation. And bed so early. I mean ... at seventeen, you shouldn't have to go to bed every night at ten o'clock. Specially not on a ship when everyone's dancing and having fun...' She paused, breathless for a moment.

Bob was looking at her oddly. 'Doesn't she seem happy to you?'

Sally tossed her head to get the hair out of her eyes.

'That's what I can't understand. It isn't natural at seventeen to be so meek and mild and...'

'Her grandmother only does it to protect her,' Bob said.

Sally glanced at him quickly but he was not smiling.

'From what?'

'The male species,' Bob said gravely. 'Mrs Ester wants to keep Beryl pure and innocent so that she can find her a wealthy husband as she did for Louella. Very rich men usually like biddable young wives—Mrs Ester believes and so...'

'But how horribly cynical of you,' Sally

cried. 'You think Mrs Dunn married for money?'

'No, but Mrs Ester saw to it that her daughter met Vincent Dunn at a moment when he was very vulnerable. His first wife had died in a car accident and he was a lonely man. Mrs Ester drew out her savings and sent Louella to stay in the same hotel...'

Sally's cheeks were hot with anger. 'I'm sure Mrs Dunn...'

'Knew nothing about it and fell in love with Vincent,' Bob said quietly. 'I'm not blaming Louella, Sally, nor even Mrs Ester. When you've been as desperately poor as the Esters have, no holds are barred. Now she is looking for a suitable husband for Ryl...'

'For whom?'

Bob grinned. 'I meant Beryl. But that's why she clucks round her like an anxious hen.'

'I still don't think it's right...' Sally began.

Bob put his hand lightly on hers. 'What time does Beryl go to bed?'

'Ten o'clock. Her grandmother tucks her up.'

'And then goes to bed?'

'Yes.'

'With a sleeping pill?' Bob said quietly.

Puzzled, Sally nodded. 'Yes, she says she can't sleep without one.'

'Then round about eleven o'clock, say to me "Beryl"—in case I forget.'

'But why...?'

Bob Chart chuckled. 'You'll find out why, then. Drink up and let's go and see if the dancing has started. I hope you twist...'

'Not very well,' Sally confessed.

He laughed down at her as they stood. 'You'll soon learn.'

Only a few couples were dancing, most people were sitting in the booths, drinking and talking. Sally knew a moment of nervousness as she went into Bob's arms. He was so tall and she hadn't danced much...

Right from the first moment, everything was all right. He led well so that she seemed able to sense what step he was going to do next. In a moment, she was caught up in the magic of the rhythm, could forget her fears and relax and enjoy every moment of the dance.

That first dance was the start of the happiest evening of Sally's life. Bob introduced her to the other officers and allowed each one a dance, but every time the dance finished, there was Bob, waiting for her, to take her back to the small secluded table he had got.

Sally's cheeks were flushed, her eyes like stars, her shining hair swinging as she danced.

'Enjoying yourself?' Bob asked.

'I've never had such a wonderful time,' she confessed.

'You should have been doing this all the trip,' he said, a faint note of reproach in his voice.

Sally hesitated. 'I—I don't like leaving Mrs Dunn alone and ... and by the time she goes to sleep—well, I feel like turning in.'

He whirled her round until she was giddy. 'I can't understand why you haven't made friends on the ship.'

'I'm afraid I don't make friends easily.'

'But why not?' he demanded. 'We've become friends quickly, haven't we? It hasn't been so hard, has it?'

Once again Sally hesitated. 'No, but ... but this is different.'

'Why is it different?' he demanded.

Sally looked up at him and was startled to find how close his face was to hers.

'Because ... because you're doing this to help me.'

He stared down at her, an odd look in his eyes. 'You honestly think I am spending the evening with you just out of the kindness of my heart?' he asked.

'Aren't you?' she asked in turn.

He spun her round and round, not answering her. As the music came to an end and they all stood and clapped, he looked at his watch.

'Eleven-thirty. You forgot to say "Beryl" to me,' he said.

'So I did. I'm sorry...' Sally confessed.

31

She had completely forgotten Beryl, Mrs Dunn, and everyone except Bob.

'It doesn't matter. Drink up and we're on our way...'

She knew a chill moment of disappointment. Was the wonderful evening already over for her? But obediently she finished her glass of cider and walked out to the deck with him.

Again a beautiful moon, slashing a wide silver path across the dark sea.

'I wonder how you'll like life out here,' Bob said casually, his hand very lightly touching her elbow as he guided her to the stairway.

'I think I'm going to love it,' Sally told him. 'The wonderful sunshine—'

'It can be too hot. Mosquitoes...' Bob warned.

Sally laughed. 'I can take it.'

They had climbed up two decks. Sally looked round curiously. This was the sun deck. Where was Bob taking her? His hand on her arm, he led the way towards a doorway. As he opened it, she heard music. The music of the teenagers, the music she loved, with its dramatic beat, its strange sad cry that set her feet moving at once. She saw a smallish room, packed full of boys and girls, twisting, laughing, talking, while a radio-gram gave them the music.

A wave of joy swept through Sally. So the

wonderful evening was not over. She watched some of the dancers—and a girl danced by, jet black hair swept up into a tight chignon on top of her head, her mouth a scarlet slash, her eyes heavily shadowed, her lashes long and thick. She wore red and green patterned silk slacks and a white lace blouse. Sally stared at her, seeing something familiar in the face. At the same moment, the girl turned her head and looked at Sally and for a moment, there was such dismay and anger in the girl's eyes, that Sally was shocked.

The next moment, the girl had danced by, lost in the smother of swirling dancers.

Bob Chart's hand on Sally's arm tightened and he pulled her backwards through the door, gently closing it, leading her to two chairs placed near the rails.

'Well?' he said.

Sally was still dazed. 'It couldn't be ... but...'

'Well?' Bob repeated sharply. 'Did you recognize Ryl?'

'Ryl?' Sally could only repeat, glad of the chair as he pulled it forward.

'Ryl after ten, Beryl before ten o'clock,' Bob said.

'Then it was Beryl?'

Bob laughed. 'Of course it was.'

'But she's supposed to be in bed asleep.'

'So what?'

Sally hesitated, battling with confused thoughts.

'If her Gran knew ... or her mother...'

'What could they do? The girl's committing no crime,' Bob said. 'What amused me was your sympathy for Ryl. She's always done this, I gather. Outwardly meek and docile, inwardly a rebel. D'you blame her?'

Sally drew a long deep breath. 'Of course not. I never could understand how she stood such a life, but...'

'I came up here once and found her,' Bob said. 'We danced. I thought what a nice girl she was. She told me the whole story. Her mother is terrified of Mrs Ester. Apparently Louella was always dominated by her mother and that's why Louella handles the children so lightly. Too lightly, I think. She still hasn't thrown off the yoke of her mother's possessive, dominating love for her. I doubt if she ever will. It will have to be something pretty important in Louella's life—some choice she'll have to make. Anyhow, Ryl—she uses that name away from home—early learned that if there was to be peace in the household, her grandmother must be allowed to think she was getting her own way. I gather Ryl is a past mistress at the art of sneaking out of houses when she's supposed to be asleep.'

'But it must be hard to lead a double life.

34

Suppose someone gave her away?' Sally asked.

'Who'd be mean enough to?' Bob asked. He twisted to stare at her. 'Don't tell me your conscience is pricking?' he said, his voice surprisingly hard. 'What harm is Ryl doing?'

Sally twisted her hands together unhappily. He was right, of course, but...

'Shouldn't her mother know? I mean, Grand-dad didn't mind me going out anywhere, so long as he knew where I was.'

'But her mother does know where she is. She's on the ship.'

'Wouldn't her mother understand?'

Bob let out a loud dramatic sigh. 'Her mother is dominated by her mother. What would happen, is that Louella would have a fight with Mrs Ester over the whole thing and Mrs Ester would win and Ryl would be Beryl for the next four or five years. This way, Ryl has the chance to develop her own personality, to make friends, to enjoy life, and yet keep the peace in her own home and help her mother. Honestly, Sally,' Bob said, sounding exasperated. 'You amaze me. You act and think like a mid-Victorian school-marm. What right have you to judge Ryl? Why, a short time ago you were sympathising with her...'

'I do—I am...' Sally said unhappily. 'But seventeen isn't very old and...'

'Don't worry about Ryl, she was born old,' Bob said. 'That girl's got more brains and common sense than any girl I know. She's had to have to get by. Otherwise her life would have been a misery. This double life of hers makes her mature and able to cope with difficult situations...'

'But...'

Bob stood up and pulled Sally to her feet. His hands were hard on her shoulders.

'Are you going to be a Judas?' he asked sternly. 'What right have you to judge Ryl? Betray her? In a few days, she'll be with her father. She said he'll understand. This double life of hers will end, then. What is it that worries you?'

Sally hesitated. 'I hate deceiving people.'

'You never deceived your grandparents?'

Sally fidgeted under his firm hands. 'I...'

'You see?' Bob sounded triumphant. 'Sally, watch out or you'll become an unbearable prig. Judging others for what you've done yourself. Oh, doubtless you can justify your own actions. It was to spare them pain, to keep them happy. But isn't Ryl's reason the same? Are you going to tell her mother?'

Sally looked up at him. 'No, but...'

'But?'

She moved. 'Don't worry,' she told him. 'I won't tell Mrs Dunn.'

His hands held her prisoner. 'But...?' he

repeated.

She looked up at him. 'I don't blame Beryl at all. I guess I'd have done the same with a Gran like hers but...'

'Sally, you've got some strange idealistic ideas, you know. You live in a dream world of perfection. Louella Dunn doesn't love her children—that's why they can't confide in her. They love her but she loves only one person in the world...'

'That's not true...' Sally said angrily, trying to wrench herself free from his compelling, imprisoning fingers.

'It is true,' Bob said firmly. 'Louella loves her husband. That's the only person in the world who matters to her. Years of giving way to her mother to keep the peace have conditioned her, so that now she lacks the nerve or personality to stand up to her—but Vincent will always come first in her life. That's why Beryl can't talk to her mother. Look, Sally...' His voice changed. Became gentle, almost pleading. 'Grow up, there's a good girl. If you drift through life believing that all mothers adore their children and all children should tell their parents everything, you're living in an artificial world. You see your parents, whom you never knew, through rose-coloured glasses. Probably if they'd lived, you'd know better. I love my parents dearly but we fight all the time. They want to dominate me and I won't be...'

'But you became a doctor,' Sally said sharply.

He grinned suddenly. '*Touché*. It seemed the easiest way out and I was tired of fighting at the time; in any case. I don't really dislike being a doctor. I enjoy my work. It's just that my dream...'

'Aren't you the one who's unrealistic?' Sally demanded. 'How many people have the chance to make their dreams come true?'

Bob grinned. 'You will.'

'You don't know my dream...' Sally said angrily.

'Don't I?' Bob gazed down into her brown eyes. 'I can tell you. A nice little house in some suburb, a placid loving man who'll work his fingers to the bone to buy you a washing machine and a T.V. set, four little children...'

Sally gave a violent twist and escaped from his hands. 'And what is so wrong with such a dream?' she demanded.

He caught hold of her again but this time his hands were not on her shoulders. His arms were round her, holding her tightly, as he bent down towards her.

'There's nothing wrong with it, Sally,' he said, his voice suddenly gentle. 'Some lucky man is going to have a wonderful wife one day.'

His mouth was on hers—gentle, then demanding. His arms were tightly round her—yet she did not fight. She made no attempt to get away as she felt her whole body relax, felt her mouth respond—and then suddenly, she was free and they were staring at one another—their eyes shocked. Sally's face was white.

So this was love. The wonderful exciting thrilling love they sang about. This frightening impulse to hold Bob close to her, to close her eyes and forget everything but the feel of his mouth on hers, his arms round her.

'I'm tired,' she said breathlessly. 'Thanks for a ... a nice evening, Dr Chart. Goodnight...'

'The night is young...' he said, looking down at her. 'Must you go?'

She nodded dumbly. Whatever happened, he mustn't know how she felt. This sweet yet frightening breathlessness, this weakness of her knees, this longing to throw herself at him and tell him that never had she felt like this before...

He turned away. 'I'll dance with Ryl, then. 'Night,' he said curtly.

Somehow, Sally made her way down to her cabin. Luckily, the other girls were always late so she had the place to herself. Thrusting her burning face into the pillow, she remembered all that had happened. The things Bob had said, the way he had looked. But always she came back to the humiliating end of the evening. Had he sensed her love for him, she wondered. Had he felt the way she returned his kiss? Had he wondered why she had let him kiss her for so long? Was he laughing, now? Was he amused because she had betrayed herself, she thought anxiously. Did he know how much she cared—how terrible it was to know that in a few days time they would say goodbye, never to meet again, she asked herself.

How could she bear it? If only she could crawl into a hole and not see him again. Surely he had only to look at her to know how she felt. Was this what he had meant by the word 'predatory'? Was that why he made no attempt to persuade her to stay with him—why he said at once, that he would dance with ... with Beryl? He had said Beryl had more common sense than any girl he knew. That Beryl was born old and had more brains than...

Was he in love with Beryl, Sally asked herself. Was that why he had defended her so fiercely?

If only she had not gone to the dance—if only he had not kissed her...

CHAPTER THREE

The deck was crowded as the ship swung through the gap in the reef and they could see the yachts moored in the harbour as a swarm of canoes came out to welcome them.

Louella Dunn was in her wheel-chair, her face flushed, her eyes bright as the ship came closer to the quay and she could see the crowd of people waiting to welcome them. She looked as elegant and perfect as usual, Sally thought, in her shantung suit of pale lemon, and the shady hat that threw a shadow on her face. Sally's hands were gripping the ship's rail as she gazed in wonder at the island before her. This was Tahiti—a magic sounding word. Something to dream about and plan for without much hope, yet here she was.

She gazed at the tropical beauty, and at the crowded quay with swarms of people, girls in bright print dresses with wreaths of flowers round their necks. Palm trees everywhere, and the strange smell that drifted to them as the big ship moved in very slowly ... It was all so different.

Sally kept her eyes fixed on the scene ahead although she knew there was no real danger of seeing Bob. He had bade the family a formal farewell earlier in the day and

41

Sally, seeing him making for them, had quietly vanished. Later, she had been told by Louella Dunn that Dr Chart had sent best wishes and his hope that she would enjoy her new life. How sorry Sally had felt then, that she had slipped away, but since that wonderful night that had ended so disastrously, she had been careful to avoid him. Not that it had been difficult, she realised, for it had also struck her that Bob Chart was avoiding her! Perhaps already he was regretting that kiss, fearful lest she had read more into it than he meant.

Standing close by Sally were the Esters, Mrs Ester regal in an elaborate dark crimson lace suit, her hat half-hidden by an enormous bunch of artificial flowers. Mr Ester was standing, legs apart, frowning a little as he smoked his pipe, elaborately waving the smoke away every time his wife tossed her head in annoyance as it drifted towards her. Johnny, Mrs Dunn's youngest child, was a thin pale boy in a grey flannel suit. He looked hot and miserable as he gazed curiously at the island. What sort of school would he go to on the small island on which they were to live, Sally wondered. Mrs Dunn had said her husband had promised her that there was an excellent teacher at the school, but would there be enough companions to help the boy grow out of his quiet shyness? Although Sally had done her best to make friends with him, there was something wary and reserved about the boy and he had never responded as she had hoped. Beryl had been the same, until the night Sally had seen her dancing—and the next morning Beryl had sought her out, a rather worried look in her eyes. They had talked and Sally had promised not to tell Mrs Dunn about it. Everything would be different, Beryl said, once they were with her father.

'Mum's so weak about Gran,' Beryl had said, twisting her long black hair round her hand. 'Dad'll have no nonsense but Mum'll fall over backwards to keep the peace with Gran. That's why I play along with them but now, everything will be different...'

There was so much happiness and confidence in her voice that Sally caught herself crossing her fingers behind her back. If Mr Dunn was so social-minded, so ambitious, would he have time to bother about his children? Wouldn't he leave that side of his family life to his wife? And if he did so...?

'What's the funny smell, Sally?' Johnny asked abruptly, coming to stand by her side, bringing her abruptly back from her thoughts.

'Copra, Johnny,' a voice said suddenly.

Sally turned round before she could stop herself, for she had recognized the voice. It

43

was Bob Chart! She felt her face grow hot as she saw the amusement in his eyes as he looked at her briefly and then down at the boy.

'What's copra?' Johnny asked.

Bob Chart, immaculate in a white linen suit, grinned.

'Copra comes from ripe coconuts, John. It's always been one of the mainstays of this part of the world. They used to do a terrific trade in it, but, I don't know why, it seems to be dying out.'

'But how do you get it?' Johnny persisted.

'When the coconuts are ripe, they fall to the ground. That reminds me, young feller, watch out they don't drop on you. Can be a pretty hefty hit for they fall from a great height,' Bob Chart was saying.

Vaguely, Sally heard his words. She was actually listening to his voice, with its deep notes, its sound of sincerity and strength. Yet he was afraid of love, and had also let his people talk him into being a doctor, when he wanted to be a sailor. Was that 'strength'? It didn't add up, or make sense, she thought. She was very conscious of his closeness to her as she leant on the rail, her eyes glued to the town before them, which gradually came closer and larger, but even as she stared at the buildings with their different pastel colours, she only saw a tall man with red hair and laughing green eyes.

44

'The nuts are collected and split,' Bob went on. 'The white meat is pried from the nuts and spread on a dryer. Actually it is usually a platform. If it rains, they cover it with corrugated iron. It generally dries in a couple of weeks and then it is sacked and sold.'

'But what's it used for?' Johnny persisted.

Bob moved and Sally, turning her head, saw the way his long fingers ran through his hair.

'All sorts of things,' Bob said. 'Fats, oils, soap. It has a strange smell. At first it is rather fascinating, then it becomes obnoxious, and then you don't notice it, at all. You learn to live with it, in time. Afraid I must go, now. Best of luck to you all...' Bob said casually.

Sally stood very still, her hands clenched round the rail. He had not even spoken to her—not noticed that he had not said goodbye. It just showed how stupid she was to have this aching inside her. Once the ship had gone, she would forget him. She had no choice. It was as simple as that.

Sally turned and hurried to Mrs Dunn's side.

'Nothing you want?' she asked.

Louella's eyes were bright with excitement. 'Nothing, thanks, Sally. Any moment now...' Her voice, normally quiet, seemed to tremble.

Sally felt rather than saw the quick look Mrs Ester gave her daughter.

'For goodness sake, Louella, don't get hysterical,' she said sharply, her voice low. 'And don't wear your heart on your sleeve. A man gets tired of such...'

Louella Dunn was not listening. She was watching as the officials began to come up the gangway on to the ship. It would be a long time before passengers were allowed ashore.

'Miss Hampton...' Mrs Ester's voice was shrill. 'Just go down and check that all the luggage has left our cabins.'

'Yes, Mrs Ester,' Sally said politely.

She hurried below. She had already been told to do this a dozen times but Mrs Ester seemed terrified that something should have been overlooked. The day before most of the heavy stuff had been collected, now it was only their hand luggage. She went from deck to deck to the different cabins. Everything had gone! Hurrying back along the corridor, she turned a corner and bumped straight into someone.

For a moment, she was breathless as hands caught her by the arms and steadied her and a familiar voice said:

'Where's the fire and why the panic?'

Bob Chart! It would have to be him. She looked up and saw a strange look in his eyes and wished he would take his hands from her arms.

'Just ... just checking the luggage,' she said. 'Mrs Ester...'

'Is a fussy old woman. I suppose she can't help it,' Bob said. He went on staring at her in a strange way. 'Why didn't you say goodbye, Sally?'

She drew a long deep breath. 'Why didn't you?' she asked.

He stared down at her. 'Where? On the deck in front of everyone?'

'What was I supposed to do? Come to your surgery?' she asked, suddenly so angry with him that she could hardly speak.

He grinned at her. The grin she could never forget.

'Might have been an idea. Have a good time, Sally, and remember one thing...' he told her.

'What?' she asked bluntly. Was he going to remind her about the kiss? Had he realized how she had felt—noticed how she had responded to the touch of his mouth? Was he going to warn her not to think that every kiss meant love eternal and wedding bells?

He gave her an odd look. 'That you're a very pretty girl,' he said abruptly, his hands falling away from her arms. 'Goodbye and good luck. May your dream come true...'

He was already walking away as Sally called out: 'I hope your dream does, too, Bob.'

47

He turned with a quick wave of his hand. 'It will, thanks. 'Bye.'

She hurried up on deck and found Mrs Ester in a panic again.

'You've been so long, I was worried...'

At last things began to move and before long, they were going down the gangway, Mrs Dunn's chair being deftly manipulated by one of the officers. Sally saw Mrs Dunn's face grow pale and dull with disappointment as a tall, thin girl with jet black hair, cut in Egyptian style, with a long fringe and hanging straight to her ears, wearing glasses with very thick black rims, and a simple grey frock, came towards them.

'Welcome, Mrs Dunn...' this girl said, her voice dull. 'Mr Dunn was unable to meet you.'

'Miss Wynne ... he's all right?' Louella Dunn said, her voice unsteady.

A brief smile flashed across the girl's dull face.

'In perfect health, Mrs Dunn.'

The girl's name was Rosalie Wynne, Sally learned as a result of the introductions that followed and she was Mr Dunn's P.A., translated, apparently, as Personal Assistant, for she was more than a mere secretary and indeed, as she later told Sally, she had her own secretary and several typists. A strange girl, Sally thought, for she spoke in a pedantic manner, her voice absolutely flat

48

and without expression, yet every now and then, she seemed to come to life and her dull eyes sparkled and her voice changed.

'Mr Dunn wondered if you would care to spend the night in Papeete?' Rosalie Wynne said to Mrs Dunn. 'I have arranged for a suite for you at the hotel but if you prefer to come out to Mahane Island right away, I can also arrange for a schooner to take us.'

'I'd like to go to the Island right away,' Louella said at once.

The girl seemed to hesitate. 'You're sure it will not be too tiring for you, Mrs Dunn? Your husband expressly said...'

'There's nothing the matter with me,' Louella Dunn said irritably. 'I've simply got to rest and...'

'Exactly,' the girl murmured. 'Then I'll arrange for you to be driven round Papeete as it is rather unusual and when you return, we'll have lunch and then go to Mahane Island.'

Papeete was indeed an unusual place, Sally thought, as with the rest of the family, they were taken in carriages round it. The horses wore strange-looking caps with bells on them, the driver was a big fat Tahitian with a broad grin and a habit of whistling out of tune which annoyed Mrs Ester very much, judging from her expression. Sally was in a second carriage with Beryl and Johnny.

There was a strong smell of copra

everywhere and Sally thought Bob had been right when he said that it was something you would have to learn to live with. The streets were crowded, with carts, cars and cyclists as well as straying pedestrians all hopelessly mingling. There were Tahitians on every corner selling flowers of fantastically bright colours. Old men walked along thoughtfully, many with wreaths of white flowers round their necks.

They had all been greeted with these wreaths as they landed. The flowers were exquisitely lovely and their scent strong. Mrs Ester had refused to wear one but the rest of them, even Johnny, wore the *leis*, as they were called.

There were lots of small stores with Chinese men at the stalls—above them were rooms with washing hanging at the windows. Most of the buildings were painted with a faint wash of colour. But the most noticeable things were the bicycles, ridden by Tahitians balancing enormous parcels on their heads. Everywhere, Sally saw palm trees. Somehow in her mind, they had always been linked with romance. Well, she was seeing plenty now, she thought, but where was the romance!

The big ship dominated the harbour but soon it would be gone and Bob would have walked out of her life for ever.

'Look at that church,' Beryl said suddenly,

as the horse slowly trotted along the uneven road.

Sally obeyed. The church had been painted white but the roof was obviously made from coral and there were green ferns sprouting from it.

Everything was so different. The people they passed looked carefree and happy in their easy-to-wear clothes and their flowers. There was nearly always the sound of music, men twanging guitars, girls singing, and always the faint sweet scent filled the air. So much to see yet Sally knew that the unusual beauty was wasted on her. She could only think of Bob—no matter, how she tried to shift her thoughts from him, again and again she found herself remembering things he had said.

Back at the luxury hotel for lunch that even Mrs Ester admitted was wonderful, Sally thought Louella Dunn looked tired, and wondered if they ought to spend the night in Papeete, but Mrs Ester was already saying that and Sally could see how it was upsetting Louella.

From somewhere, Sally found courage.

'I think Mrs Dunn would rest more easily in her own home,' she said unexpectedly.

Louella smiled gratefully. 'Yes, Sally, that's just how I feel. I've been longing to see it and ...'

'All right,' her mother said, 'but don't

51

complain if you're exhausted.' She looked at the silent Rosalie Wynne. 'Will the water be rough? Should I take travel pills?'

Rosalie's face remained expressionless. 'It is unusual for travellers to feel sick on this short journey but if you anticipate feeling ill, it is a good idea to take precautions.'

Sally found herself wanting to laugh. Was Rosalie putting on an act? Secretly laughing at them for taking her seriously? Rosalie was in her twenties, surely it was an extraordinary way to speak, Sally thought.

The schooner was a big one and comfortable chairs were found for them all. Sally tried not to look at the big liner in the harbour as they sailed out through the gap in the reef.

'Goodbye, Bob,' she thought, and the ache inside her seemed to grow into a vacuum of emptiness. Someone had once said: 'It is better to have loved and lost, than never to have loved at all,' but whoever it was must have been bats, Sally told herself angrily. If this was love, this painful longing, this constant recalling of everything both of them had said, this regret at having said something, or because you hadn't said something ... What pleasure was there in it? Just this aching desolation...

She looked back at Papeete—the town was receding fast. But now she could see the mountains, the palm trees crowding to the reef, the many lagoons, the sands all different colours, she noticed. Some yellow, some white, the sand in one cove was even black. The tops of the mountains were hidden by drifting clouds, but the sky was a cloudless blue, and there was always the lovely sun to warm them.

They passed many islands on their way across the calm, beautiful water. Each one seemed more lovely than the last but Rosalie kept saying:

'Wait until you see Mahane Island. Now, that is really *avant garde*.'

Sally wondered what she meant but did not like to ask. Feeling restless, she wandered round the schooner and was leaning against the rail when Rosalie joined her. Rosalie seemed to lose some of her affectedness as she spoke to Sally.

'How d'you get on with Mrs Dunn?' she asked abruptly.

Sally turned to stare at the girl with the odd blank face.

'I like her very much,' Sally said warmly. 'She's kind and most generous.'

'How did you come to get this job?' Rosalie asked.

Sally told her briefly. 'And it's been a wonderful experience,' she finished.

'H'm,' Rosalie said, looking sceptical for a moment. 'I had the impression that you were unhappy.'

Sally felt her cheeks burning and wished that Rosalie's dark eyes were less shrewd.

'That has nothing to do with Mrs Dunn,' she said.

Rosalie smiled briefly. 'I see. Usual story. Shipboard romance. When you've travelled as much as I have, you won't waste time on heart-break. Keep free, no emotional entanglements and you'll stay happy.'

'But how...' Sally began and stopped.

Again that brief smile. 'You'll learn,' Rosalie said. She hesitated. 'Why did the Esters come along?' she asked.

Sally confessed she did not know. 'It was all arranged before Mrs Dunn offered me the job.'

Rosalie was narrowing her eyes as they passed an island with two cone shaped mountains.

'It's a pity,' she said tersely. 'It's going to be difficult enough without them around. Mr Dunn didn't invite them, I know that!' She turned to look at Sally. 'How d'you get on with them?'

Sally hesitated. 'I like him very much but...' she replied and remembered with a pang of misery that those were the words she had used when she answered the same question put by Bob.

'He's a honey,' Rosalie said, apparently forgetting her meticulous use of pedantic words. 'But she's a ... horror. Anyhow

54

Vincent will...' Rosalie stopped speaking and looked momentarily dismayed. 'Golly, I must watch my tongue I mean Mr Dunn will cope.'

'What's he like?' Sally asked.

'All right,' Rosalie said curtly. 'Very nice to work for but stuffy at times. Very keen on protocol—everything must be just perfect. But he's nice. I've worked for him for five years and he's a good boss.'

'We'd better join the others,' Sally said. 'Or Mrs Ester will think we're plotting something.'

The walked down the sloping deck—the water was so calm there was little movement—to the group reclining in chairs. Johnny was sound asleep, mouth open, looking absurdly young and vulnerable. Beryl was leaning forward, watching the antics of some flying fish by the side of the boat. Mr Ester was smoking with a happy smile on his face. Mrs Ester was reading a book, her mouth a thin line of disapproval and Louella Dunn was asleep. But noticing the way Mrs Dunn's fingers were moving as her hand closed and opened, Sally knew that she was only feigning sleep—probably as a protection from her mother's perpetual moans. A warm flood of sympathy filled Sally. Poor Mrs Dunn. It was bad enough to be forbidden an active life for six months without having trouble between her mother

55

and husband. Was that, perhaps what she dreaded, and why she was so highly strung?

Suddenly Rosalie pointed. 'There's Mahane Island...' she cried.

Louella Dunn's eyes opened instantly. Even Johnny woke up, yawning and rubbing his eyes as they all gazed at the mist-hidden mountain that loomed up ahead. They were still far away but they could see the shape of the island perfectly. It was L-shaped and the longer end of it was dominated by the most enormous mountain imaginable that reached an imperative finger up into the sky, as if pointing at something. A mountain with a wide base but narrowing to the merest thread of a pinnacle. As the schooner slid through the water, they began to see more.

Sally could see small lagoons, half hidden by palm trees—caught a glimpse of what looked like a township of small buildings and then, on a plateau as if dug or hollowed out of the side of the mountain, she saw a house. She wanted to laugh—it looked so out of place in that setting. It was a modern house, tall, narrow, and apparently made of glass. In the sunshine, a million windows seemed to sparkle.

'It's very modern...' Rosalie said proudly. 'We have everything. Our own electricity plant—luxury.'

'My husband built it?' Louella Dunn said slowly, as if surprised.

56

Rosalie turned round. 'Yes. It was designed by a young architect who came out to the South Seas and became a beachcomber,' she said. 'Mr Dunn found him and gave him a chance to salvage his career.' She waved her hand. 'This is the result.'

'It must have cost a great deal of money,' Mrs Ester said disapprovingly.

Rosalie looked at her. 'Of course, but only the best is good enough for Mr Dunn.'

'But how did you get the materials?' Mrs Ester demanded.

Rosalie looked blank. 'They were delivered by ships.'

'It looks very odd in such a setting,' Mrs Ester went on.

Louella Dunn was smiling, her face young and happy. 'Perhaps that is its charm,' she said.

Now the island was growing bigger and bigger as they came closer. Sally could see several big cars parked by the side of a wharf and, glancing at Louella, saw the way her eyes were shining. That vacuum of loneliness seemed to swell inside Sally again as she knew envy—deep cruel envy. How wonderful to be married to a man for eighteen years and still know the joy and excitement that Louella Dunn so obviously knew. Sally closed her eyes for a second. That was how she would have felt for Bob, if she'd been married to him for eighty years, she thought unhappily. If it was true that you only loved properly once, then her life stretched ahead of her, empty and desolate.

'There he is...' Louella said suddenly. 'He looks well, Rosalie.'

'That is what I said,' Rosalie said, her voice slightly arrogant.

Sally opened her eyes in time to see the strange look Mrs Ester was giving her son-in-law's P.A. A look of distrust, dislike and disapproval. It seemed to ooze out of the elderly woman's face with its pursed mouth.

The schooner docked smoothly and let down a gangplank. The first man to walk up was a tall man with black smooth hair. He wore a light tropical suit with a white silk shirt and a grey silk tie. He walked straight to Louella, hands outstretched.

'My dear,' he said, in a deep voice. 'It's been such a long time...'

Louella Dunn's face was radiant. 'Vincent ... darling.'

Vincent kissed her lightly on both cheeks, still holding her hands, and then straightened to look round.

'Hi, young feller,' he said to Johnny, gently flicking his fingers against the boy's cheek. 'You're going to have a great time here. Underseas fishing, mountain climbing, the lot...'

'He's a delicate boy,' Mrs Ester chimed in.

58

Vincent turned to her with a courtly bow. 'I beg your pardon. I should have greeted you. Unpardonably rude of me, Madre. It's very pleasant to see you. I hope you had a good voyage.' Before she could answer, he turned to George Ester and held out his hand. As they shook hands, Vincent Dunn said warmly, 'You're looking well, George.'

'I'm not too bad,' George Ester said with a big grin. Obviously, Sally thought, they were good friends. 'Could be worse,' he added with a wink.

And then Vincent Dunn turned to Beryl, who was waiting patiently, her eyes like stars.

'Dad...' she said and flung herself into his arms.

He gave her a hug and then held her away, looking down at her demure blue silk frock and the matching band round her long black hair.

'What's happened to the jeans and flapping shirt?' he teased.

'She's passed the tomboy age,' Mrs Ester chimed in. 'Now she wears decent clothes—clothes that a well-brought-up young lady...'

'Too bad,' Vincent Dunn murmured and looked at Sally. 'You must be Sally Hampton. My wife wrote and told me about you. Welcome to Mahane Island...' he said, holding out his hand.

Sally shook hands, liking the firm touch of

his fingers, the smile in his dark eyes, the real warmth in his voice. He was quite the most handsome older man she had ever seen. He was lean with the toughness of an athlete. He was scrupulously clean and tidy, even in the hot sunshine.

Then he turned to his P.A.

'Rosalie,' he said, his voice changing to crisp authority, 'I'll take Mrs Dunn and her parents with me. Will you bring the children and Sally?'

'Of course, sir,' Rosalie said quietly.

Soon Sally and the others were in a big grey car and driving away from the group of tall, obviously new buildings round the small quay. As they drove along the road which immediately began to climb the mountain in long curving loops, Sally saw the thatched houses built high up on stilts. On the porches of many of them, she saw old women, weaving. Sometimes an old man was braiding what looked like ropes. Swerving round a steep corner, they passed a pool by the side of the road. Three girls were lying by the side of the water, their toes dangling in it, creamy flowers tucked behind their ears, gaily coloured strips of silk wrapped round their bodies. They lifted lazy hands in greeting as the car sped past and the driver, a lean Polynesian called Tajuka, waved so violently that the car swerved for a second.

The car with the Dunns and Esters in it had sped ahead but Rosalie had told Tajuka to drive slowly so that they could enjoy the scenery.

'Isn't it too absolutely gorgeous?' Rosalie said, her voice unusually warm as she gestured with her hand.

'It's just as I imagined it,' Beryl said fervently, her eyes bright with excitement.

It was indeed beautiful, Sally thought. Dense masses of trees and bushes clothed the mountainsides ahead of them. Everywhere she saw waterfalls—crystal-clear water falling down the side of the rocks into pools filled with lilies. Now and then they caught a glimpse of the blue ocean—or of a lagoon with the white surf pounding against the surrounding reef. There were many thatched houses on stilts, sometimes they saw a small naked boy fishing in a pool. Once they caught a glimpse of a group of Polynesian men dancing to the sound of twanging guitars. And all the time there was the sweet scent of flowers.

'You either adore this place or loathe it,' Rosalie said.

'I'm going to adore it,' Beryl said promptly.

'Me, too,' Johnny chimed in. 'Dad'll let me do anything. He never fusses...' he said proudly.

Rosalie looked at Sally. 'And you?'

Sally's smile felt stiff. 'I think it's out of this world,' she said truthfully. 'A dream place,' she added, and then wished she hadn't said the word 'dream' for it reminded her of Bob.

Now they could see the fabulous building made of glass just ahead of them. A narrow tall building, it was surrounded by a garden that was ablaze with scarlet, orange and purple flowers. The lawns were smooth and green. There was a terrace facing the sea and Sally caught glimpses of striped umbrellas.

Inside, it was even more startling. Doors that slid back into walls to disappear, windows that could be opened up and down, sideways, or even slantwise. Rosalie showed them their rooms. Luxurious to Sally's eyes. Lofty; painted strange shades of silvery grey with sudden splashes of colour. She, for instance, had a violet rug and the palest blue coverlet to her bed, curtains of a glass-like silvery material and the most wonderful view of the ocean, stretching far to the horizon, a shimmering translucent blue.

For a moment, she was alone with Rosalie.

Rosalie chuckled as Sally said, 'I've never seen such a house.'

'Nor had we. First time Mr Dunn saw it, he nearly had a fit. However, the architect talked us into it. Now he's making a name in New York for himself. He took a film of this place and it seems to have sold him.'

'It's got everything,' Sally said slowly, looking round. There was a heater for chilly days—if ever there were any here! A fan for hot days. Her own shower. 'I can't get over it.'

Rosalie laughed. 'I can see you don't know Vincent Dunn. Only the best is good enough for him.'

'But it must have cost a fortune.'

'He's a very wealthy man and likely to be even wealthier if this comes off,' Rosalie said.

'This?'

Rosalie smiled. 'We're here to investigate some weird legend of hidden treasure. Already we've found a new kind of mineral that is making Vincent Dunn another fortune, if we find the treasure, as well...' She gave a little whistle. 'The sky's the limit. Now have a shower and change and come down to drinks before dinner.'

'Mrs Dunn...' Sally said.

Rosalie smiled. 'Don't panic, you're not shirking your duties. Here she'll have her own personal maid—as you will, too, for we all do—and your job will be that of companion and peace-maker.'

'Peace-maker?' Sally echoed, puzzled.

Rosalie's eyes were amused. 'Yes, keeping the peace between the Esters and Mr Dunn. I can't suggest how you do it but if a way isn't found, then there's going to be trouble. And the one who'll get hurt is Louella

63

Dunn...' she added, closing the door softly
behind her as she left the room.

CHAPTER FOUR

Sally had barely started to unpack with the
aid of Tehutu, a young Polynesian girl, who
was to be Sally's maid, when a message came
to her to go to Mrs Dunn.

She found Louella Dunn nearly in tears.
Sitting before a dressing-table that had
three mirrors, Louella was gazing at herself
miserably as a tall Polynesian girl brushed
her hair.

'Oh, Sally!' Louella said, her voice
relieved. 'Please show Kaha how to do my
hair. She hasn't a clue...'

'Of course,' Sally said, taking the brushes
in her hand and smiling at the tall girl with
the sullen mouth and sultry eyes. 'This is the
way Madame likes it, Kaha...' she began.

As she demonstrated slowly, carefully
explaining each step, Sally was getting a
glimpse of the beautiful room. The luxury
almost took her breath away. It had been
furnished for a beautiful woman with
love in every thought, Sally told herself
wonderingly. The deep pile of the white
carpet, the exquisitely graceful gold silk
curtains, the embroidered cover to the bed,

the deep built-in cupboards that lined one side of the wall, showed that. There was the same wonderful view from the window that Sally's room had.

At last, Louella Dunn's hair was swept up into the intricate pattern she liked in the evening.

'I want to look my best, Sally,' Louella Dunn said, almost apologetically.

Sally smiled. 'You always look lovely,' she said.

A faint colour filled Louella's pale cheeks. 'I'm growing older every day,' she said sadly.

'You look as if you're growing younger,' Sally said firmly. 'You look quite different tonight—alive, sparkling and so happy.'

Louella Dunn laughed gently. 'I am, Sally, so very happy...' The door opened suddenly and Mrs Ester stood there.

'Of course you'll have an early night, Louella,' she began, and stopped as she saw her daughter's elaborate hair style, the blue silk gown on the bed.

Louella smiled. 'I've lived for this night for a year, mother. I'm not going to miss it,' she said quietly.

Sally saw the hesitation on Mrs Ester's face. 'You may be right, Louella,' she began. 'But don't be too lively or he'll think this...' She waved her hand expressively towards the wheel-chair, 'is made up.'

'He knows it isn't,' Louella Dunn began

65

indignantly and then seemed to remember that Sally was with them. She gave the girl a smile. 'Thanks for coming to the rescue, Sally. I think Kaha understands, now. Go and have a shower and change into something light. Vincent tells me the evenings are always warm, here.'

'They have trade winds...' Mrs Ester said. 'I hope we don't get bronchitis.'

Sally had an irresistible desire to giggle for nothing was ever perfect in Mrs Ester's eyes. She turned away quickly.

'Thank you, Mrs Dunn,' she said formally.

In her own room, she found a bath waiting for her with delicious fragrant bath salts in it, and her clean undies were laid out in readiness. Tehutu was hanging up the last of Sally's clothes and turned with a friendly smile.

'*Aué*' ... Tehutu said in an awed voice, gently fingering a lime silk frock. '*Vahine* very lucky.'

Sally smiled, wondering if *vahine* meant girl. She decided to wear a very light batiste frock; it was a salmon pink with a gold thread running through it.

Tehutu beamed approval. '*Aué* ... ' she said again. 'Very pretty frock.'

Sally went to soak in the deliciously hot bath. How lucky she was, she told herself for the millionth time and then caught her breath. The last hour had been so full of events that she had not had time to think of Bob. She glanced at the clock. What was he doing now, she wondered. Had he got time off and gone ashore? Or was he in his little surgery, tending people's woes? For that, Bob had told her, was what most of the ailments on board ship were. Fortunately, he had added, it was rarely anything serious, though he had to be prepared for any emergency.

Now as she dressed, with Tehutu's aid—how odd it seemed, Sally thought, to have your own maid when for the past few weeks, she had been virtually Louella's maid—she wished with all her heart that she was back again in Papeete, on the big white ship, with the chance of seeing Bob, even if he didn't see her. The feeling of emptiness seemed to grow as Tehutu brushed her hair, holding it up in her hands and letting it fall lightly, an approving smile on her face. And as Sally went down the wide staircase to the big reception hall below, she felt more like crawling into bed where she could weep in peace, than being gay.

Mr Dunn came to met her, his dark eyes approving as he looked her over.

'I hope you'll be happy with us,' he said, his deep voice sincere.

Sally looked at him and smiled. 'How could I be anything else?' she asked. 'In such a lovely place and with such nice people.' Even as she said it, she wished she had not. Did it sound rather forward, she wondered anxiously, or 'smarmy'? She had not meant it to, for it was the truth.

Vincent Dunn smiled. 'Thank you, Sally. I'm glad you've come to join us.'

Louella Dunn was in her wheel-chair, scintillating, laughing gaily, talking. A little too gaily, Sally wondered with momentary uneasiness, as she looked at the beautiful woman. Was Louella trying too hard, Sally thought. She glanced at Mr Dunn and saw the smile he gave his wife and some of Sally's anxiety vanished.

The Esters were sitting together. Mrs Ester stiffly, her glass held away from her, a slight look of disapproval on her face. George Ester was enjoying himself, cheeks flushed, voice jovial as he told Vincent about some of the people on the ship.

'The queerest crowd. Can't think where some of 'em get the money,' he was saying.

Beryl was there too. Still wearing the dress she had worn on the ship. Her eyes were shining like stars but she sat quietly, hands meekly folded. Sally noticed that Vincent Dunn kept giving Beryl little puzzled looks that he tried to hide. Rosalie, Sally gathered, had a flat of her own in the staff buildings.

'I think she sees enough of me during the day,' Mr Dunn said, with a chuckle.

Sally saw Mrs Ester's quick glance at him and the way her mouth was pursed.

'Much more suitable, Vincent,' she said. 'It never does to mix business with friendship.'

Vincent Dunn laughed. 'How right you are, Madre.'

Dinner was a delicious meal, served expertly and by obviously experienced servants. Afterwards, Beryl was dispatched to bed by Mrs Ester and Sally rose, as well.

'If you'll excuse me,' she said politely to Mrs Dunn.

'There's nothing I can do?'

Vincent Dunn laughed. 'No, thanks, Sally. I'm here to see to that, now.'

Sally was glad to get to her own room, to close the door. She went to the window and stared at the ocean. The moon was just rising in the black sky and the stars beginning to twinkle. She stood very still, pressing her hands against her mouth, trying to will herself not to feel the empty misery, not to ache with longing to go back to Papeete, to see Bob.

He had walked into her life, and out again even more swiftly, she told herself. He feared marriage and love because ... Because...? Her thoughts skidded to a standstill. Because he was afraid his dream would not come true? Wasn't that a selfish outlook, she wondered. And suddenly she knew the truth.

It was not a selfish attitude, it merely showed one thing—that Bob Chart had never really been in love.

She knew, beyond shadow of doubt, that if Bob walked into the room and asked her to follow him to the back of beyond, even if it meant leaving all her friends, her grandfather, giving up her dream of a home and children ... anything he asked, she would go because life without him wasn't life—it was mere existence.

Hastily she undressed and got into bed. Would she ever sleep, she wondered unhappily. It was quiet and yet there were strange noises. A rustle as the palm trees moved before the wind. The distant roar of the waves on the reef. Suddenly there was a shrill piercing noise like a swarm of hornets. A strange noise...

She awoke to find Tehutu by her bed with a tray. Tea and a delicious crisp roll, already buttered, and a glass of orange juice.

'Breakfast is ready when you would like it,' Tehutu chanted in a sing-song voice, her eyes bright. 'I run your bath?'

Sally stretched herself luxuriously. 'Thank you, Tehutu.'

After she had bathed, she put on a white frock and hurried downstairs. Only the Esters were eating breakfast.

'Ridiculous,' Mrs Ester was saying. 'Every doctor gives the same advice. A good

70

breakfast is essential. Vincent should know better than to take the children out on an empty stomach...'

George Ester burst out laughing, coughed and choked, his face bright red as he regained his voice.

'Really, my dear, I can't see Vincent balancing the children on his empty stomach.' He began to laugh and choke again and Sally had to turn away to the sideboard where eggs and bacon, sausages, and fish were kept warm on small warming stoves, so that Mrs Ester did not see her smile.

'George, you know very well I did not mean that,' Mrs Ester began.

Sally sat down with her plate of bacon and eggs, very conscious that Mrs Ester was watching her.

'Sleep well, my dear?' George Ester asked.

Sally smiled. 'Like a log, thank you, Mr Ester.' She looked at Mrs Ester. 'Rosalie told me that Mrs Dunn had her own maid and would be looked after but has she had breakfast?'

Mrs Ester gave a little sniff. 'Everything has been attended to, Sally. We are no longer needed.'

The fact that she had called Sally by her Christian name told Sally a lot more about Mrs Ester than the elderly woman would have imagined. It showed Mrs Ester's

71

distress, that she was hurt, denied the right to care for her daughter. In fact, was no longer needed. Sally felt sorry for the elderly, thin, unhappy woman yet surely a husband should come first, she thought.

'In addition,' Mrs Ester went on, her voice trembling a little as if she was trying hard to contain her anger, 'Vincent has taken both the children out at some unearthly hour to ... to indulge in underwater swimming...'

Mrs Ester's voice and expression condemned the sport as some deplorable, rather shocking exercise and again Sally found it hard to hide her laughter. George Ester made no attempt.

He guffawed loudly. 'Oh, come off it, old girl,' he said. 'Vincent hasn't seen his kids for a year. Can you blame him for giving them a bit of fun?'

'It's cold early and no one should go out without first eating breakfast,' Mrs Ester said severely.

Sally finished her meal and as quickly as she could with politeness, excused herself and hurried up to Mrs Dunn's room. Louella Dunn was still in bed.

She smiled at Sally. 'Sleep well?'

Sally smiled and said, 'I had a wonderful night. This is a gorgeous place, Mrs Dunn.'

Louella's face clouded a little. 'I think so. I wish ... I wish...'

The door opened quietly behind Sally.

72

Vincent Dunn stood there. He looked lean and healthy and in a good mood as he smiled at them both.

'Well, Louella,' he said cheerfully, 'Johnny is thrilled with his new life. I'm taking him to meet Paddy Masters later this morning. His new tutor,' Mr Dunn explained. Turning politely to Sally he went on: 'Would you come and see me in my study in half an hour?' he asked. 'I'll just go and have breakfast with the kids,' he said, and turned and left the room.

Sally knew a wave of fear as the door closed. Was he going to tell her that her services were no longer needed and he would arrange for her to return to England? She realized with a shock that she wanted to stay on Mahane Island, for at least, it was in the same part of the world as Bob. While she was here, there was always the vague chance that he might either visit the island or she get the chance to go to Australia...

She caught her breath with dismay. Was she already planning to chase him? Wasn't that, she asked herself what he expressly dreaded. Was that what he called a predatory female?

Louella was smiling at her. 'Don't look so terrified, Sally. Vincent only wants to brief you as to your new duties and to ask you if you want to stay with us.'

Sally felt herself relax. 'Of course I do,' she

73

said quickly. And then she hesitated. 'I hear he's a perfectionist. Perhaps I can't...'

'Sally...' Louella lifted an admonishing finger. 'Positive thinking, please.' She smiled. 'Vincent is a perfectionist but he has patience and is prepared to train his staff. You should have seen Rosalie when she first came to work for him. She was all arms and legs, wore too much make-up, her hair was all frizzed—teased, I think they call it, and her clothes! She had no taste, at all. But Vincent said he could see she had something he needed—the qualities of loyalty, ability to work hard, interest in other people, and personality. He says you have the same...'

Sally's cheeks were hot. 'I ... I...'

Louella laughed. 'Run along, Sally. He's a stickler for punctuality.'

Downstairs, Sally found her way to Vincent Dunn's study. It served as an office, also. He was signing letters and asked her to sit down. She obeyed, hands folded neatly as her grandmother had taught her. She looked round. It was a luxurious room yet designed for work. Files hidden behind satinwood panels, several 'phones, a tape recorder.

'Relax, Sally,' Vincent Dunn said, his dark head bent over his desk. 'I won't be a moment.'

Sally tried to obey, looking round at the satinwood panelling, the heavy curtains that framed the wide window, the glimpse of the garden she could see from where she sat.

He pushed the papers aside and looked at her. His face, that could be stern, came to life and he moved his hands as he spoke.

'Sally, my wife is very fond of you. You've been good to her—given her companionship and affection as well as service. As you see, the latter is not necessary, here. We have an excellent staff under an exceptionally good American housekeeper so the house runs on oiled wheels. You all have your own personal maids. But Louella still needs loyal companionship and someone to cheer her up in her fits of depression. She has a feeling of uselessness, at the moment, poor girl. Of being a burden. I want her to play a large part in my social life. You can help her there.' He paused. 'Sally, we need you but if you prefer to go back to England, there'll be no arguments. That was the arrangement.' He looked at her.

Sally drew a deep breath. 'I'd like to stay, please.'

He smiled and his face was almost radiant. 'I'm glad, Sally. Now, I trust you so I'm being absolutely frank. As undoubtedly you know for Louella never hides it, the Esters were very poor when Louella was young. Probably that's why Louella feels so insecure. Certainly it is the reason for her mother's behaviour. Mrs Ester is terrified of being left penniless, despite the fact that considerable settlements have been made on the Esters, as well as, naturally, on my wife and children.'

Mr Dunn's voice had become formal and sounded as if he was angry but it changed again as he continued:

'I love my wife, Sally, even though at times I find her hard to understand. But then, I remember her past and I can forgive her. Unfortunately I find it harder with Mrs Ester. I cannot always be so tolerant even though I understand her reasons.' He gave a little sigh. 'It isn't always easy to live with your in-laws.'

'I can see that,' Sally said. And then wondered if she had been too outspoken.

But Vincent Dunn did not look annoyed. 'I want you to act as a buffer, Sally. Let me explain,' he went on. 'I am not asking you to be a spy...' He smiled at her. 'Simply my agent, in a way. I want my wife to be happy and I value our marriage but...' He paused and got up, walking to the window, talking over his shoulder.

'I find this hard to explain, Sally. Madre has a habit of swooping on me and demanding certain prohibitions of the children's actions with which I find it impossible to agree. I like to be prepared so that I can handle it diplomatically and so keep the peace.'

He turned to look at Sally, smiling

ruefully. 'I'm not a quick thinker and have a bad habit of losing my temper. That upsets my wife. She wants us both to be happy and her loyalty to each of us tears her in two.'

He swung round to look out of the window again. 'I admire Mrs Ester very much, Sally. I know she made a great many sacrifices for her daughter to give her a good education and a chance to make a success of her life. On the other hand, I love my children and consider I know how to bring them up without instructions from...' His voice was uneven for a moment. 'I know she means well but...'

He turned to look at her, walked across the room, bringing a chair, straddling it as he looked at her, his voice grave.

'Sally, I'd appreciate it if you would warn me if any trouble is hovering. If, for instance, Mrs Ester decided to disapprove of Paddy Masters. Let me know as soon as possible and I can be diplomatic about it.' He smiled. 'Does it sound very weak, Sally? Maybe I ought to tell Mrs Ester the truth—that in-laws should not live with their married children.'

Sally hesitated. She remembered Johnny's eagerness to get to the island and how he said everything would be different because his father never fussed. She told Mr Dunn this and saw the pleasure on his face.

'He's been molly-coddled this last year,'

he said.

Sally nodded. 'Mrs Ester is convinced Johnny is delicate and is always warning him about getting over-tired or too cold. Johnny isn't too delicate, I'm sure. He's just at the age when he's growing suddenly. He's young but he needs friends. Mrs Ester, apparently, won't let him play games or mix. He had a tutor in England and...'

'I know...' Vincent Dunn hesitated. 'It is deplorable but like so many aspects of my mother-in-law's behaviour understandable.'

He stood up and began to walk about the room restlessly, his face grave and expressive as he explained: 'You see, the Esters had a son, Sally. He was five years older than Louella. When he was fifteen, he was badly injured in a game of rugger and consequently died.'

Sally stared at him in dismay. 'How terrible...'

'Exactly. It explains Mrs Ester's fear complex about games and rough handling by other boys. Paddy Masters, who runs the local school, will cope with Johnny and see he mixes with boys and gradually learns to defend himself.' Vincent Dunn gave a wry smile. 'We can't protect our children for ever, Sally. We have to teach them to look after themselves. I dislike what appears to be deceit but what Madre doesn't know, won't hurt her.'

The words reminded Sally of Beryl and she found herself telling Vincent everything—about the clothes Beryl had to wear, the right chaperonage Mrs Ester maintained—or thought she did—on the ship, and the second life Beryl lived.

Sally's cheeks were burning. 'Maybe I sound a prig but I hate children having to deceive their parents...'

Vincent Dunn sat down with a rueful smile. 'I agree. It shouldn't be necessary but unfortunately most of us do it. I think it is a sign of independence, a proof that we are growing up and thinking for ourselves. After all, if we always do exactly as we are told, what are we to do when there is no one there to tell us what to do?' He laughed. 'Thanks for telling me, though. I will handle the situation diplomatically.'

'I think Beryl is going to tell you herself,' Sally said, her cheeks hot. 'I feel mean telling you. I promised not to...'

'Tell her mother?' Vincent Dunn supplied the rest of the sentence. 'I'll give the child a chance to tell me so don't worry.'

'I ... I could never make out how Beryl managed it,' Sally said impulsively. 'I did her packing and never saw the clothes ... I mean her "Ryl" clothes as she calls them. She hates the name of Beryl...'

'I know. Unfortunately it happens to be Madre's second name and Louella wanted to

79

please her. Maybe we could call her Ryl in future, it has a certain unique charm...' Vincent Dunn said thoughtfully.

Suddenly he began to laugh. 'Sally—here's a father hoist on his own petard. I've just remembered that years ago, I told Beryl that my suitcases all had false bottoms and in that way, I managed to hide things from my parents. I'm glad the child had gumption and savvy enough to act that way. Shows she has character.' He looked pleased as he spoke. 'I like my children to think for themselves, even if we don't always agree.' He gave a sudden little sigh. 'You know, Sally, the children are good. Like us, they don't want to upset their grandmother because that upsets their mother. You may find this hard to believe but I have known Louella cry for days after I argued with her mother...'

Sally hesitated. She was tempted to ask if that was healthy—but she had no right.

It was as if he read her thoughts. 'No, Sally, it isn't healthy,' he said gravely. 'I wanted my wife to see a psychiatrist years ago but the mere suggestion sends Mrs Ester off in a tizzy.'

He smiled wryly and she smiled as well, for the word sounded strange on his lips.

'Mrs Ester accused me of suggesting that her daughter was mental and off we went, more scenes, more tears. A vicious circle.'

He stood up. 'Sally, that's why I need your help. This illness or whatever it is...' He waved a hand expressively. 'Is purely due to my wife's emotional discord. I want to ward off as many assaults on her nerves as I can. May I rely on you?'

'Of course.' Sally stood up, thinking it was the end of the interview. To her surprise, Mr Dunn told her that in her new position, her salary would naturally be increased. He mentioned a figure that staggered her.

'I...' Sally began.

Supposing she could not do all the things he required of her, she thought worriedly. 'I've never been a social hostess...' She looked at him unhappily. 'I never know what to talk to people about...'

He smiled. 'My dear child, just remember that it is your duty to make my guests feel welcome. You'll soon learn how to pay the adroit compliment—if it is a man, to laugh at his jokes and let him feel how witty he is. If a woman, compliment her on her beautiful gown, or the colour of her hair...' His eyes were twinkling as he looked at her anxious face.

'Believe me, Sally, I am not telling you to be a hypocrite. Look at every guest and try to find something admirable about him or attractive about her. Then let the guest see that you've noticed this. Compliments are rare and I think we all respond to them.

They give our morale a little needed boost and help us over bad moments. Realize that many guests are shy and need encouraging. If you think that, it'll help you from feeling shy yourself.' He smiled. 'Don't worry, I have faith in you. Go and bask in the sun, Sally, and enjoy life. Our first party is tomorrow night. Rosalie will brief you.'

Feeling slightly dazed, Sally obeyed. She went out on to the wide paved terrace and sat down in one of the chairs under a slanting red and white striped sunshade. How beautiful it all was, she thought, relaxing her tensed limbs, gazing at the blueness of the lagoon below—the reef against which the surf was pounding, throwing up great masses of sparkling water which fell heavily on to the coral.

Sally closed her eyes, planning the letter she would write to her grandfather about her new life. How he would love the perpetual sunshine, she thought, watching the graceful dancing movement of the palms in the slight breeze, and the colour of the flowers. Such brilliant crimsons, purples and yellows. The grass so green and smooth as velvet. That lovely tree of huge creamy white flowers whose fragrance kept drifting towards her.

'Sleeping?' a voice said, startling her.

It was Rosalie. The same dull lifeless eyes, black hair whose fringe almost touched the top of her dark glasses.

'I've got to brief you, I hear...' she went on.

Sally got up hastily. Rosalie was wearing an extremely well-cut suit of natural shantung.

'This way...' Rosalie said, turning away to walk round the tall narrow house with its amazing number of windows flashing in the sunlight.

Rosalie had a small blue car. When Sally commented, Rosalie gave her an odd look.

'I have to get around and it's quicker than waiting for an official car and a driver. I expect you'll get one, later,' she said.

'I can't drive...' Sally said.

Rosalie looked at her. 'You'll learn. I'll probably have to teach you.' She gave a wry smile. 'I don't envy you. I have a fiendish temper.'

Sitting by her side as the car flew along the curving road down the mountain, Sally noticed that Rosalie had dropped her pedantic way of speech.

Now they were driving through miles of sugar cane and pineapple and Rosalie told her something of the life there.

'These guests of Vincent ... I mean, Mr Dunn,' she corrected herself crossly, 'are mostly important influential people. Mr Dunn has lots of pies into which his fingers go. He is a very wealthy man but he never seems satisfied and is always starting

83

something new. He isn't a happy man...'

'He isn't?' Sally said, startled. She had been watching a tall good-looking Polynesian strolling along the road. He wore a red *pareu*—she was beginning to learn the names of things, she realized—and a garland of leaves in his hair. He looked happy and relaxed.

'Mr Dunn unhappy?' Sally repeated.

Rosalie swung the small car round a sharp incline. Straight below them as the car circled, they could see a sheer drop down the mountainside to the lagoon.

'How can he be happy with a wife like that?' Rosalie asked. 'She's always ill or miserable. Fancy a woman with a face like Louella's and a husband like Vincent being tied by apron strings to a woman like her mother.' Rosalie's voice was scornful. 'If Louella doesn't watch out, she'll lose her husband.'

'He loves her...' Sally began indignantly.

Rosalie gave her an odd look. 'Maybe now but a man only has so much patience and Mrs Ester is wearing it very thin.'

They were down on the level now, the little car spinning along as Rosalie went on:

'Funniest thing is that Mrs Ester is terrified of that very thing happening and yet she could be the cause.' Rosalie turned her head. 'Might be an idea to let the old lady know that you have a true love, Sally. Maybe

84

then she won't watch you with suspicion.'

Sally's cheeks burned. 'Why should she?'

'Search me,' Rosalie said, shrugging her shoulders. 'She never stops watching me. That's why I put on an act with her. Bored with life, sadly disillusioned, uninterested in the male gender...' Rosalie said with a sudden smile. 'Boy, am I interested in them!' she laughed. 'Didn't you think I talked oddly?'

'I did...' Sally confessed.

Rosalie laughed. 'I got tired of her bright eyes watching me every time I talked to the Boss.'

'You mean, she thinks Mr Dunn...' Sally began, shocked.

Rosalie's laugh rang out. 'Louella's marriage means security for them all as well as status value. Haven't you seen what a snob the old lady is? Yes, she's scared lest any of us draw Mr Dunn off the straight and narrow path...' She laughed again. 'She should worry if she saw some of the beauties that come here in yachts. We're just not in the same class, Sally. They're out of this world...' Her voice was envious.

She braked and stopped the car. Below them in the big lagoon, there were fishermen at work.

'It's fascinating,' Rosalie said quietly. 'Just watch...'

Sally obeyed. Against the background of a

cloudless blue sky with tall palm trees gracefully tossing their fronds down towards the water, stood the fishermen. Each one stood far apart from the next and soon Sally saw why. The nets were circular, Sally guessed about a width of six feet. The man draped the net over his arm and looked down into the crystal clear water—as soon as he saw the small fish, then with one quick movement, the fisherman would catapult the net.

What a picture it made, Sally thought, as she saw the net spread in the air into its full shape—then fall on the water and sink.

'There are small weights fastened round the edge,' Rosalie explained. 'That makes the net sink and the fish fall into the pocket.'

She began to drive on. Now they were driving on the level but turning inland, going round the base of the strange mountain. Looking up at it, it seemed like a silver glass at the end, so narrow was it, Sally thought. It had a strange fascination like everything on the island, she realized. Now they were driving along an avenue of giant ferns. It was very close and humid and through gaps in the ferns, they caught glimpses of scarlet flowers.

When they reached the group of modern buildings which were, Rosalie explained, staff offices and housing, Sally was amazed at the difference in her companion. Rosalie's eyes sparkled, her voice was gay and yet crisp with authority. Sally's head ached with trying to remember the names of the men and girls to whom she was introduced. The men all wore the apparently standard shorts and vividly coloured shirts. The girls wore mostly straight shifts, bright and very clean. Everyone seemed friendly and cheerful but Sally gave up trying to sort them out or even to try to remember what work they did.

Mr Dunn seemed to have a very large staff but later, as Rosalie drove her back to the glass house, Rosalie said they were under-staffed.

'You'll like working for him, Sally,' she said, and Sally was glad to notice that Rosalie appeared to have quite accepted Sally as a friend. 'He's tough, demands the earth, but he appreciates it. That's what we like.'

She pointed out to sea. 'Sorry you're not on that?' she asked.

Sally caught her breath. She recognized immediately the white outline of the *Aurora*!

'Mr Dunn's very clever,' Rosalie was saying, her voice sounding far, far away. 'He's given the Esters a suite of their own. That'll give the Dunns a little privacy. He thought up a good reason...' She chuckled. 'You see, he likes to dine late. Never before nine o'clock, and Mrs Ester prefers to dine at seven o'clock, otherwise her digestion is impaired,' Rosalie said, her pedantic voice returning for a moment.

Sally was no longer listening. She felt lifeless, frozen with misery, her hands clasped in her lap tightly, her nails digging painfully into the flesh. The *Aurora* was moving so slowly and with such stately grace, with such relentless cruelty, too, Sally thought miserably. It was carrying Bob away from her, out of her life forever. How could she bear it, she wondered.

Rosalie glanced at her curiously. 'Golly, I'm sorry,' she said sincerely. 'I forgot your boy friend was on the boat. Don't let it get you down, Sally. I know it feels pure murder at the moment but always remember, they're as good fish in the sea as jump out of it.' She gave an odd little laugh. 'Cheer up, Sally.'

Rosalie put her foot down on the accelerator and the little car leapt forward, going round a curve in the road that shut the ocean out of view. Sally sat very still, her eyes now tightly shut.

'Oh, Bob,' she was thinking miserably. 'Why did I have to meet you? Why? Why? WHY?'

CHAPTER FIVE

Bob Chart was on the sun deck as the big ship moved away from Papeete. He was conscious of a strange feeling of desolation as he watched the laughing crowds who were waving goodbye, tossing long coloured strings of paper and shouting last moment comments. He walked away from the passengers and stared at the mountains which were half-shrouded by drifting mists. Why did he feel such strange unhappiness? Never before had he known this feeling—it was almost as if he had lost—or thrown away—something valuable, he thought.

He told himself not to be a sentimental fool, and plunged down below to his surgery. There was plenty of work waiting for him there.

It was several hours later that he went up on deck again, still absurdly miserable. He saw a group of people crowding round the rail and joined them. They were staring at the most peculiar-looking mountain he had ever seen. The island was not big and it was L-shaped but it was the mountain that caught one's attention. It was on the longest part of the island and started as a massive block of rock but as the mountain reached up towards the sky, it seemed to become thinner. Finally, it was merely a thin spiky finger, across which drifted clouds. The whole island had a strange mystical look which held an odd fascination for him. He was startled when someone touched his arm and he turned and saw a girl by his side was smiling at him.

'That's Mahane Island...' she said in a friendly voice.

Bob frowned a little. He knew her face vaguely as that of one of the passengers he usually tried to avoid. The clinging, predatory type—once you got in their social clutches, your life on board was doomed to an everlasting round of cocktail parties, dinners and bridge drives. He hated that kind of routine life. But the unusual misery that filled him had returned and he felt the need to talk.

'Is there something special about Mahane Island?' he asked.

The girl laughed. 'That's where the Dunns were going...'

'The Dunns...' Bob echoed and suddenly he understood. 'Oh, the Dunns,' he repeated, his voice coming to life.

He looked at the island again. So that was where Sally was! How close it looked—yet that was a fallacy! He knew that his sudden urge to jump overboard and swim to the island was not only ridiculous but impossible. The ocean was full of sharks, for one thing...

He found himself laughing. Be your age, man, he told himself crossly. Sally isn't the only girl in the world. You'll forget her.

'I see—that's where the Dunns live...' Bob said to the pretty ash-blonde girl by his side. He turned away and walked down the deck, climbing to the next deck where he could be alone.

He leant on the rail of the ship and stared at the island as they passed it majestically—then turned to watch the island with its strange peak until it was finally lost to sight in the mist. His last link with Sally Hampton had gone, he told himself, thrusting his hands deep into his trouser pockets.

So what? Sally was just a girl and he hardly knew her. A quiet shy girl who was very pretty but ... There were other girls, he told himself again.

Yet would he ever forget that moment when she was in his arms? How relaxed she had been, her mouth warmly responding to his kiss. And then the startled, almost shocked look on her face as they moved apart. Surely, Bob asked himself, he was not fool enough to imagine he was the first man she had kissed.

Why had he been so scared? What was a kiss? Especially on board ship! Kisses were two a penny, there, everyone knew that.

Why had he been scared? Why had he

thought at once of what is known cynically as 'the tender trap'? Sally was not the type of girl who was on the look-out for a husband. Besides, one kiss...

Why was he scared of love, Bob asked himself, and knew the answer. His long dormant dream of sailing round the world would be squashed forever. Sally was not the type of girl you could play around with. With her, it would be the real thing or nothing. He had been scared, let's face it, he told himself. So he had avoided her for the rest of the voyage to Papeete and now she was gone forever...

Already the tropical twilight was descending, throwing long dark shadows on the deck, making him shiver, though not with the cold.

After all, Bob asked himself, trying to be logical, what was he making all this fuss about? He had met a pretty girl, liked her and kissed her once. So why the fuss if he had avoided her afterwards? What could he have done? Suppose he had said that he loved her? How could he know that was the truth, he asked himself.

One kiss meant nothing. What could you learn from one kiss? Yet he had known. Beyond shadow of doubt, he realized. That strange catalyst no one can analyse had made his skin tingle, filled the air with electricity and he had known he loved Sally as he kissed her. He had known, too, from the look in her eyes as he released her, that Sally knew she could love him, too.

So he had run away...

He turned abruptly and went down to his cabin. No sense in wallowing in self-pity, he told himself. He would soon forget the girl!

One thing, he would have plenty to do for the rest of the voyage and by the time he reached Sydney, he would be too excited at the prospect ahead of him, to have time to waste on a girl.

★   ★   ★

He was on deck as the liner approached the Heads that stood at the opening to Sydney Harbour.

The many pictures he had seen had never done justice to it, he thought, as he looked at the buildings that crowded down to the water's edge, the glimpses of gracious houses on slopes of velvet-like lawns, the hills covered with trees, the skyscrapers. The harbour was alive with craft of every size.

There was so much to watch, he thought, as he stared at the yachts racing by, their sails every colour of the rainbow. Navy blue, yellow, as well as sails with red and white stripes added to the brightness.

Everything looked as if it had been freshly scrubbed. He stared ahead, waiting for his first glimpse of the Bridge ... When it came into sight, breath-taking, incredibly graceful, he thought again how unsatisfactory mere pictures were.

The Bridge dominated everything—towering high above them. The liner moved along with majestic slowness and the decks were lined with passengers, laughing, talking, beginning to wave as the Circular Quay, and the big modern shipping terminal which was packed with waiting people, came in sight.

Bob turned and hurried down to his cabin. He had a lot of work to do for he would have to clear up and hand over to his successor in a few days and then he would be free. Free to make his dream come true...

He bent his head over the books and wondered why he felt so depressed. Wasn't this the beginning of something he had dreamed of for years? Why must he remember Sally with her swinging fair hair that had made his hand ache to stroke it? Her shy yet happy eyes, that funny little nose. Why couldn't he forget her?

Suddenly he began to laugh—only there was no mirth in his laughter. He had always sneered at sentimental pop songs, yet they were right, every time.

He began to hum: 'I've got her under my skin...' and then, furious with himself, slammed the ledgers shut and stalked up on deck, talking to anyone he met, determined to exorcize the ghost of Sally from his mind.

*　　　*　　　*

A few days later, Bob was free. Free to walk ashore and see how the Bridge dominated every part of the fast-growing city where skyscrapers seemed to spring up out of the ground overnight and the old buildings, rubbing shoulders with the new, seemed to know that their days were numbered. It was a strange city, full of life. He was startled to find the streets so narrow, the traffic so fierce. Yet he could not find it in his heart to blame the motorists, for some of the pedestrians deliberately provoked the drivers and invited death.

He found the small terrace houses fascinating with their wrought iron balconies, especially those with tenants who painted the walls and doors bright colours, adding window boxes and striped blinds to the gaiety.

He walked round Hyde Park and stared at the harbour from there. How beautiful and serene it was, he thought. He went on a harbour cruise and marvelled anew. There was some quality about Sydney that vaguely reminded him of London but he could not place it.

He took a train out to one of the distant suburbs where his old friend, George Soar

95

lived.

He looked at the slummy districts the train rattled its way through—it was like all big cities—the dingy small houses, the big factories, the narrow roads, the washing on the rotating clothes lines, washing that must be dirty the instant it was hung out because of the smog in the air. But as the train left the first suburbs behind, the vista changed and gradually the houses grew bigger, the gardens more ambitious, the roads wider, the trees greener. The train rattled on a bridge that crossed an estuary, with tree-clad hills and small houses half-hidden and calm water with men rowing and fishing.

George Soar was waiting on the platform. Bob was startled as he saw the brown sun-tanned face of the tall man with the lean body and quick curious glance. George had changed in the years since they had met.

Bob thought what a fool he was. All men change in eight years. He probably had. He did not look as lean or fit as George did, and he certainly did not have that wonderful tan.

The heat of Sydney, to which he could not get used, hit him as he stepped out of the train. The two men shook hands.

'My word, it's good to see you,' George said warmly.

Bob grinned. 'I'll say. You look a proper Aussie ... Where did you get that tan?'

George shrugged. 'Because I sail a lot, I

guess. Play golf. Also my job as salesman for fertilizers takes me out a great deal. Car's waiting...'

Bob was duly impressed with the big Mercedes car and even more impressed with the large single-storied house George drove him to.

'By the way, Bob,' George said, 'don't call it a bungalow or my wife'll slay you.'

'Thanks for warning me,' Bob said.

Elsa Soar was a good-looking girl with dark curly hair and a sun-tan Bob knew most English girls would give anything for. She was friendly and matter-of-fact and produced a colossal meal. Afterwards they talked.

Bob looked round the very modern kitchen with its electric stove, enormous refrigerator, cupboards, double sink, etc., and separate laundry containing a washing machine and spin-dryer.

'You've got a lovely house,' he said. George Soar must be earning a fabulous salary, he thought.

The tall lean man grinned. 'It's not ours yet and won't be for another thirty years.' He leaned his elbows on the table and laughed. 'We have a plan, Bob. Interested?'

'You bet...' Bob, comfortable in a folding chair, crossed his legs. Elsa Soar was gathering the dirty crockery and taking it to the sink. Bob noticed that George made no move to help her.

'Elsa and I both earn good salaries,' George said, waving his cigar vaguely. 'But it costs a hell of a lot to buy a house like this.' He named a figure that took Bob's breath away. 'We're also saving for the yacht. The one we want is going to cost the earth and our year round the world won't be cheap...'

'I appreciate that...' Bob began. He felt a little uncomfortable, sitting there while Elsa did all the work, but she seemed content and was listening with a smile.

'I'm looking forward to it,' Elsa chimed in. 'My word, we'll have fun.'

Bob was startled. He looked at her. 'Are you coming along?'

Elsa's face was bright. 'You bet your last dollar I am. Think I'm going to let George loose in a world of gorgeous girls?' She laughed. 'Ask George. I'm a darned good sailor.'

'She is, too,' George said complacently. 'I taught her. Boy, did she used to be sick at first. I laughed my head off when she turned green...'

'But I got my own back, too,' Elsa interrupted. 'Remember the Manly Ferry that day...'

George rocked with laughter as he told Bob the story.

'You can get quite a swell, crossing the Heads and it took me by surprise. Elsa earned the laugh but bless her, she didn't even smile...' George's look at the girl standing by the sink did something strange to Bob.

It made him feel horribly alone. As though he was in a hostile world with no one who cared if he was sea-sick or not. No one to smile at him as Elsa was smiling now at George. No one—at all.

As the days passed, Bob's loneliness seemed to become intensified. He learned a lot about the Soars. They reckoned on five years to build their yacht—during those years both would work like slaves during the week, work even harder over the weekend on the yacht they would build in their backyard. At the end of the time, they would launch their yacht, let their house...

'You can get fantastic rents,' George said. 'Probably get thirty pounds a week for this place furnished.'

'A week?' Bob gasped.

Elsa joined in. 'There are masses of wealthy country people who'd jump at renting a house near the city like this. We'll have no difficulty. That'll take care of our regular payments and also pile up something for when we come back at the end of the year. Then we're starting our family. I want two boys and two girls...'

'I want six,' George said. 'Three of each...'

They were laughing and looking at one another again in the way that always made Bob feel peculiar. For a moment he knew envy. The sort of envy he had never experienced in his life. How lucky they were. Everything planned ahead, some goal to work for. But not alone for they were partners and the hard work was fun. Never once had he heard Elsa moan about having to do housework at night, nor complain because at weekends he and George went off on their own, nor grumble because they were often late for 'tea', as they called the evening meal, for if Bob met George in the city, they invariably had a session in the 'pub' on the way back.

Bob was realizing something. He had dreamt of his yacht and trip round the world but he had done nothing constructive about it. He had some money saved but it was absolutely nothing to the amount George said they'd need.

'It's got to be a good ship,' George said firmly. 'We want no fun and games with a woman aboard.'

'Is it wise to take Elsa?' Bob asked tentatively.

George looked at him as if he was mad. 'Elsa's tough. She'll be useful.'

Bob faced facts. He'd have to get a good salary and save hard if he was to be George's partner in the planned project.

It was not too difficult to find a job and he took a post as 'locum' for a busy doctor in one of the suburbs nearer the city. He stayed at a small private hotel and worked harder than he had done for many years. The doctor's practice was a big one and the salary was good but Bob seemed to spend most of his time driving the car to different, rather seedy, boarding houses and treating an innumerable number of Italian, Greek and Portuguese immigrants. Some of them could not speak English. Luckily languages had been Bob's favourite subject and he soon learned to pick up enough phrases to get by.

He was shocked at the way some of the immigrants lived but he realized that to them, it was sheer paradise. Even though they lived, often several families in one room, in circumstances he couldn't have borne, yet he knew that to them it was luxury after their own home conditions.

Soon he learned that it was this type of immigrant who made money in Australia. The families worked for nothing, their profits—for most of them started out by buying a small shop—being ploughed back into the business. When they could, they would buy another small shop, and another, and so on, *ad infinitum*. Bob learned to respect and admire the immigrants for their ability to work hard, their grateful acceptance of this new life and the opportunity to make a good living, and give their children the chances they never had.

He also learned that their main, and almost sole, grouse was the Australian's insistence on calling them 'New Australians'.

One man spoke gravely to Bob about this. 'They expect us to be naturalized yet never are we accepted. I know a fine man. Lived here thirty years, has three sons, all doctors, and yet when he lost one of them, the papers called him an immigrant, and "one of those New Australians". How long must we live here to be accepted?'

Bob worked hard and long, spending his weekends with George and Elsa sailing, agreeing that Elsa was 'tough', each time feeling a little more lonely and envious when he left them. He was thirty-one years old, he told himself, and what had he to show for those wasted years? True, he was a doctor, but he had allowed his whole life to be embittered because of his own failing—because he had lacked the courage to tell his parents the truth, for he knew it would disappoint them to know he wanted to break away from the family tradition and become a sailor instead of a doctor.

He was feeling very humble, these days. His vivid memory of Sally haunted him. Why had he been such a weak fool as to lose a girl like that, he asked himself. If George and Elsa could make a success of it—and look how happy they were!—wasn't there a good chance that he and Sally could do the same? It needn't destroy his dream. It hadn't hurt George's; indeed, Elsa's enthusiasm had acted like a flame to George's dream and might have been just what he needed to make him do something constructive about it.

One Sunday, lying in the sunshine on Manly Beach, Bob happened to read an advertisement. Normally he did not read adverts, for he could get another 'locum' job when his present one ended so he was not worried.

It was the big black letters of this advertisement that caught his eye:

'MAHANE ISLAND'

The words blazed and something clicked in his mind. That was the island where Sally was! Blinking in the bright light, Bob read on. They wanted a doctor to work at the new hospital. Experience in surgery as well as medicine was essential.

Bob whistled softly as he saw the salary. On that, he could save the money he needed so badly for his partnership with George.

On the other hand ... he thought, his mind seemed to slide to a standstill. He had got over that nonsense about Sally and if he went to the island, he would only get involved and it might not be wise. Elsa and Sally were very different types—Sally would probably be horrified at the thought of going round the world in a yacht. She would want her own home and children...

'Coming for a swim, Bob?' Elsa called, jumping to her feet, her beautifully-proportioned body darkly tanned, looking even more amazing in her brief white bikini. She held out her hand with a grin. 'Race you...'

Running across the sand which burned his bare feet, Bob decided to forget the advertisement. It was the wisest thing to do.

CHAPTER SIX

Sally stood at one of the doors of the big reception room where the guests were always entertained. Rosalie was at the other door. A few guests had already arrived and were grouped round Louella Dunn, who sat in her wheel-chair, looking incredibly lovely in her apricot-coloured taffeta gown, her eyes very bright, her laugh silvery.

Sally watched her thoughtfully. They had been on the island now for several months and there was still only an uneasy peace between Mrs Ester and Vincent Dunn. It was rather like sitting on a volcano, Sally thought, for she was always on the look-out for a warning of trouble.

She could see Vincent Dunn, bending over his wife to tell her something, then straightening and turning to smile at the portly Frenchwoman by his side, saying something to her that made her look pleased.

Vincent Dunn was an incredible person, Sally was thinking, as she stood waiting for the next lot of guests. Several yachts were in the harbour and it should be a busy evening, for Vincent had many friends and they all knew they were always welcome. Sally looked down at her ivory brocade gown. Simply cut but so elegant that she felt sure everyone must know what a lot of money it cost. 'Uniform' was what the Dunns called it!

How she had changed, Sally thought, in the few months. She could feel it herself for she was no longer painfully shy or at a loss at how to greet anyone. Vincent had taught her so much, given her self-confidence, taught her to be poised.

It was amazing how deftly he handled the most difficult situations. How cleverly he had helped Beryl get rid of the childish clothes and without any trouble. He had merely congratulated Mrs Ester on her ability to help Beryl pass the tomboy stage and become a young lady, but now, he said, she would be meeting men and women from all over the world at the parties, so it might be wise for Beryl to grow up a little faster and to start wearing clothes that were more sophisticated.

Now as Sally moved forward to warmly welcome an American couple who were visiting the island in their yacht, she remembered that it was Vincent who taught her to say how much she admired the beautiful lines of their yacht and ask about their future plans. They were a good-looking couple, middle-aged. The wife was beautifully groomed, her hair immaculate. The husband had a pleasant accent that Sally could not place. As she led them along the great room to Louella's side, Sally quietly asked them what part of America they came from and discovered that friends of theirs had visited the Dunns six weeks earlier. Sally remembered them, and so could make conversation without any difficulty. After introducing them to Louella Dunn, dropping a few hints so that Louella knew the name of their yacht and where they came from, Sally could leave the rest to Louella. Glancing round before returning to the door. Sally saw that Mrs Carstairs was in trouble with Paddy Masters.

It was Vincent, again, who had taught Sally how to handle such situations and so she hurried to rescue the red-cheeked, flustered little woman.

Paddy Masters was part Irishman but used his brogue only when he wanted to be humorous. Mrs Ester called him a beachcomber, but had finally admitted that he was a good teacher. Johnny's eagerness to go to school, his willingness to do his homework—all these things had impressed Mrs Ester, much against her will, Sally was thinking. Paddy was a tall, thin man, with equally thin brown hair that was wispy, fast receding from his forehead, and having an odd habit of fluttering in the slightest breeze, as if eager to leave Paddy's scalp.

His roguish brown eyes were always kind, even when he appeared to be sarcastic, and Sally liked him. Paddy also seemed to like her and they would have long arguments which both enjoyed. Sally could never quite understand, she was thinking as she hurried to the little woman's rescue, why Beryl disliked Paddy. It seemed to be mutual for Paddy also avoided Beryl.

'Of course Polynesians are clean...' Paddy was almost shouting, his loud voice obviously embarrassing the plump little woman. Paddy had a habit of jumping on an imaginary soap box and holding forth at length on the slightest pretext. Somehow little inoffensive Mrs Carstairs, whose husband was a chemist working for Mr Dunn, had put her foot into it.

'As clean as the likes of us, I'll have you

know...' Paddy continued. 'They bathe three times a day in their streams and lagoons which is twice more than I do. Mrs Carstairs, it's you I'm after asking—how many times a day do you bathe?' he demanded.

Sally tried to run without appearing to do so. She could see the desperate look in Mrs Carstairs' eyes and she mentally scolded Paddy for teasing the poor woman.

'Sure, and they wear shoes on Sundays,' Paddy was saying, 'and why shouldn't they run about barefoot if that's the way they like it?'

'I only said I wondered their feet didn't get cut by the coral,' Mrs Carstairs said agitatedly. 'I then said it must be the dirt on their feet had made them tough...'

'And why shouldn't they be tough?' Paddy asked. 'Sure, and I know what's wrong. Like all the others, you're picking on the girls. I know they're lazy, but aren't we all, with half the chance? I know they start jobs and then drop them and wander off but at least they're not hypocrites...'

Sally reached Mrs Carstairs just in time. The plump little woman's face was bright red, now. She looked round wildly, like a hunted animal.

'How right you are, Paddy...' Sally said in the light tone Vincent Dunn had taught her to use at such moments. She slid her hand under Mrs Carstairs' arm and squeezed it reassuringly. 'I couldn't agree more. They really are delightful people. Don't you love the friendly way the children run to meet you, Mrs Carstairs? And they're always singing. But who wouldn't sing in this paradise...'

Mrs Carstairs had recovered her breath and composure. She smiled gratefully at Sally. 'It is indeed lovely. Now I must really go and talk to Mrs Dunn...'

She hurried off, looking to Sally rather like a flurried mother hen who has lost her chicks.

Sally looked up and saw Paddy grinning. 'You shouldn't tease the poor soul. She takes everything so seriously,' Sally said.

Paddy went on grinning. 'And why not, if I might make so bold as to ask you, mavourneen?' Paddy said. 'If a body bites, it must be hungry, so I was just after feeding her...' he added, with his most innocent look.

Sally had to laugh. Paddy always had that effect on her, she thought. She turned and thought she saw fresh visitors arriving so she slipped her hand through Paddy's arm.

'Come and do your social duties,' she told him, 'and try to behave, there's a darling,' she added, smiling up at him.

Vincent Dunn came across the room and Sally turned to him, with her quick smile.

'Is there something I can do, Mr Dunn?' she asked.

He smiled. 'I merely wanted to congratulate you, Sally, on your choice of frock. It suits you perfectly. You were clever to choose it...'

Sally blushed with pleasure at the compliment. She had wondered at the time if she was making the right choice, she remembered, as she had thought it might be too sophisticated for her. Every other month, a selection of frocks and gowns arrived 'on appro.' on the island, and they had their choice. They were called 'uniform' and paid for by Mr Dunn, and Sally had felt uneasy because of its high price. She was glad that he liked it.

'Thank you...' she said, stammering a little.

'She's a nice child, isn't she, Paddy?' Vincent Dunn asked with a smile.

Paddy was obviously in the mood for fooling, Sally saw. Now he struck a horrified attitude and scowled.

'Child—is it you're saying? How dare you call this lovely woman, a child. I'll have you know it is an insult, sir...'

'Oh, Paddy, pipe down,' Sally said, beginning to laugh.

It was one of those good moments, one of those moments when she felt warm and happy and the loneliness inside her vanished temporarily. Her eyes shone and she laughed and in the same moment, turned her head and saw Beryl walking in through the open door, a tall red-headed man by her side.

Sally caught her breath.

It couldn't be . . .

But it was!

It was Bob. Dr Robert Chart. He had his hand tucked through Beryl's arm and he was looking down at her, laughing at something she had said.

*   *   *

At the same moment, Bob was keeping his eyes fixed on Beryl, trying to get over the shock of the difference in Sally. She had always been an attractive girl but now there was an added glow, a sort of patina. Was she so happy?

He tried to concentrate on Beryl. She wore a black sheath, with a low-cut back and a high demure front. Her black hair was coiled elaborately round her head, her ear-rings and necklace sparkled. She looked very different from either the 'Beryl' or the 'Ryl' on the ship.

Mr Dunn had invited him to the party and he had come, steeling himself. Telling himself that it had been a momentary illusion, a figment of the imagination. That he was not in love with Sally Hampton. Just

111

because it had been very pleasant to kiss her, it did not mean 'love'. He had told himself constantly that he would remain cool, calm and collected and here was his heart pounding about inside him like a wild thing. All he could think of was that, obviously, he had not meant anything to Sally. Why, she was positively glowing with happiness.

He had been on his way in when he had met Beryl. She had whisked him off to a cool courtyard where a fountain tinkled, had got them both drinks and asked him what on earth he was doing there.

She was waving her glass about, being very sophisticated and gay. Overdoing it, Bob had thought. He happened to glance up and saw the reason. They had an audience. A man standing in the doorway to the courtyard, staring at them with an odd expression. A tall lean man without much hair and what there was of it, was ruffled and moving in the slight breeze. And then he had swung round and walked away.

It was like pricking a balloon and watching it collapse. The life and gaiety vanished and Beryl was her old unaffected self.

'It's nice to see you, Bob,' she said, and Bob realized that she honestly meant it.

'Who was that bod?' he asked, indicating the doorway.

'Him?' Beryl said lightly. Too lightly, Bob wondered. 'Oh, that's just Paddy Masters.

He teaches at the island school. An odd type. Gran calls him a beachcomber but Dad thinks the world of him. Tell me about yourself. I thought you were going to build a yacht and sail round the world. Changed your mind?'

Bob fidgeted. Took a sip of his drink and was startled at the unique tang of it.

'No, I'm still planning to do that but when I got the chance of a job at the hospital and it was good pay, I took it. I'm going to have to save a lot of money to build that yacht...' he told her.

'Oh, so you're the new doctor,' Beryl cried. 'Dad told us about you but he didn't say your name, and, of course, to him your name wouldn't mean anything.'

'How's everyone? Your mother—Johnny?' he asked.

'Johnny's in paradise. He does all the things Gran's against but she doesn't know as we don't tell her. What she doesn't know doesn't hurt. She's got a complex about games, Dad said, so it's kinder not to worry her. Paddy is teaching him underwater swimming, and judo and mountain climbing and ski-ing...' She stopped for a moment, breathless. 'Mum ... she's just the same. Always with Gran. I wish...' Beryl paused.

'And you? I see, you're out of those ridiculous clothes.' Bob had said.

Beryl laughed. 'Dad fixed that,

113

diplomatically but very definitely. I'm slowly being launched into society,' she laughed. 'Dad's wonderful. Most sympathetic.'

'And Sally...?' Bob said rather carefully, trying to keep his voice light. 'Is she still here?'

'Still here?' Beryl laughed. 'I'll say she is. Why, she's a different person, Bob. You won't know her. Dad has turned her into a swan. Not that she was ever an ugly duckling,' Beryl went on hastily. 'She was always pretty but she was so shy and quiet and so ... so school-marmish. Now she's quite different. She helps Dad and his P.A. at these receptions and looks after Mum, telling her things she ought to know about visitors...'

Beryl jumped to her feet, holding out her hands. 'Come and see, Bob. Of course, Sally worships Dad—but then all girls do. There's something about Dad that is amazing, it has the same effect on women of all ages. I've even seen a teenager fall for him. Not that he ever notices, bless him...'

As they reached the entrance to the reception hall, Bob had seen the group of men and women round Louella Dunn in her wheel-chair but he was too far away to see her expression. What he really saw, was Sally.

Indeed a different Sally. How right Beryl was. A Sally, elegantly dressed, in very high

114

heels, with pearls round her neck, wearing an expensive long gown, moving gracefully and without shyness, her hand on the arm of the man he had seen earlier, the one who Beryl had said her grandmother called a beachcomber. Sally was laughing at him, her face happy.

And now the dark-haired elegant man who had interviewed him for the post, and asked some shrewd questions, was joining them, saying something. Sally turned eagerly to look at him and something inside Bob seemed to die. Beryl was right. All girls fell for a man like Vincent Dunn. Poor unsophisticated innocent little Sally, Bob thought at once. Had she discovered yet what had happened to her?

Something that in her ethical eyes would be an unforgiveable crime.

She was in love with a married man.

*   *   *

Sally must have shown her shock in some way for both Paddy and Vincent Dunn seemed aware of it. They stayed by her side, talking to each other, giving her a chance to recover.

For one incredible moment, Sally had thought she was going to faint but time gave her the strength to get control of herself so that she could say, her voice gay:

115

'I think that's the doctor we had on the ship, Mr Dunn. The red-haired man with Beryl...'

Vincent Dunn turned his head to look towards the door. He frowned a little, his dark eyes momentarily clouding.

'Dr Chart? He didn't say he'd met my family,' Vincent Dunn said sharply.

'That handsome red-haired man with the freckles?' Paddy Masters chimed in. 'The one ogling our young Ryl...'

'He's not...' Sally began sharply, caught her breath and felt her cheeks hot as Paddy turned to give her a thoughtful look. She grabbed at her composure, keeping her voice casual. 'He's not like that, Paddy. He's a man dedicated to a dream...'

Vincent Dunn turned to look at her. 'A dream?'

Sally nodded. 'We all knew. His dream is to build a yacht and sail round the world.'

Paddy gave a soft whistle. 'Could be fun.'

'We understood he was going to live in Sydney,' Sally began.

Vincent Dunn was nodding. 'He told me he'd spent some months there. He's the new doctor at the hospital, Masters.'

Paddy looked surprised. 'Is he a surgeon, too? Think he can cope?' His voice had lost its mockery and he was looking at Vincent Dunn almost worriedly.

Sally saw the quick smile on Vincent

116

Dunn's face. 'He'll cope all right...' he said.

Beryl was bringing Bob Chart towards them and Bob was wearing the smile Sally hated. However, at least, it 'helped' for it stung her into self-defence so that she could welcome him gaily.

'Bob Chart, how nice to see you. We thought you were building your yacht in Sydney...' she began. And then thought how unnatural and affected it sounded.

He smiled. The smile she knew so well and that was always her undoing—the funny lop-sided smile that seemed to share a secret with her.

'I've not forgotten my yacht,' he said. 'But it's going to cost more than I reckoned so I've come here to save money.'

Paddy Masters was laughing. 'You'll be a clever man if you succeed, doctor. I've been trying to do the same this many a year.'

Bob gave the Irishman a strange look, almost condescending, Sally thought, and she was suddenly angry.

'Maybe I'll be more lucky...' Bob began.

'Paddy's trouble is that he's too generous,' Sally interrupted.

'Sally,' Vincent Dunn said quietly, 'just a moment...'

'Of course,' Sally said, grateful for the chance to escape, leaving Beryl with the two men.

Fresh guests were arriving and for the next

117

hour, Sally was busy. It was only as the big buffet dinner was served and everyone helped themselves to some of the delicious food on the long table, that Sally found Bob by her side.

'How are things?' he asked casually.

Sally was coping with the difficult problem of using a knife and fork with a plate held in her hands and no seat to be found.

'All...' she began.

Bob quietly took the plate from her. 'Let's find somewhere,' he said, leading the way out of the crowded room to the courtyard that Beryl had taken him to. They both sat down, everything quiet apart from the silver tinkle of water and the distant roar of voices and laughter.

'Thanks,' Sally said, as she took her plate. 'It's so much easier to eat when you've got a seat.'

Bob laughed. 'I'll say. Good food. Do you do the housekeeping?'

'Oh no. Mr Dunn has an American housekeeper who handles everything,' Sally told him.

'What do you do?' Bob asked, his eyes amused.

Sally pretended to think. 'I entertain Mr Dunn's guests, I keep Mrs Dunn company, I try to keep the peace.' She gave a little grimace. 'That's the hardest task of all.'

'Oh, Mrs Ester!' Bob said sympathetically.

118

'How are things with her?'

Sally had finished eating and put down her plate. She sat back, looking at her companion.

'I don't think it's easy for her,' Sally said slowly. 'You see, she's always been the mainstay of her family, the one who lays down the rules and keeps them together. She finds it hard to accept Mr Dunn's orders, especially as they seem to be the opposite of what she thinks is right.'

'I notice Beryl isn't wearing those stupid clothes.'

Sally smiled. 'No, Mr Dunn was most diplomatic! He congratulated Mrs Ester on keeping Beryl young and unspoiled but he said he felt that it might be wise to speed up the process of Beryl's debut.' Sally laughed. 'Honestly, Bob, he's clever. Mrs Ester purred. The same with Johnny. He's a different child...'

'And so are you,' Bob said bluntly.

Startled, Sally stared enquiringly. 'For the better?' she asked, waiting for him to tease her.

To her surprise, he didn't look at her as he answered.

'I'm not sure...' he said slowly. 'It's too soon to tell, yet.' He stood up abruptly. 'I suppose we should join the others. I mustn't forget you have your duties to carry out.'

Sally stood up. 'Yes, I'm very busy.' She

felt cold and alone. Why must he make it so plain that he did not want to stay with her? He collected the plates.

'Beryl seems happy here,' he said casually.

'Beryl would be happy anywhere, if she can have companionship and fun,' Sally began and then thought it sounded catty. Her cheeks hot, she went on: 'She's a very happy person. Actually, you know, she's helping at the school so many days a week.'

'Beryl ... a...'

'A school-marm?' Sally said coldly and clearly. 'Yes.'

Wasn't that what he had called her? He had been amused because she didn't like the thought of the double life Beryl was leading, because she was afraid Beryl might find herself in situations where she could not cope alone. But Bob had merely thought Sally was smug and had called her a 'Victorian school-marm'. It had hurt. It still did.

Bob chuckled. 'I can't see it. Isn't that Irishman the teacher?'

'Yes, and he's an extremely nice man,' Sally said.

'Hi ... steady on,' Bob said. Now he really was laughing at her. Sally saw. 'No need to bite my head off. I didn't say he wasn't...'

'No, but need you say *teacher* in that sneering voice?' Sally asked, feeling her temper rising. 'Paddy has been to Dublin

University and also Cambridge. He's a very well-educated, highly intelligent...' She stopped speaking suddenly, aware that Bob was looking at her oddly.

'Sounds as if you're in love with the man...' he said slowly.

She gave him a quick look. At least, he did not think she was in love with him! Maybe that kiss in the moonlight that had revealed so much to her had told him nothing.

'Of course I'm not,' she said crossly, hurrying, glad to be back in the reception hall where she could mingle with the guests.

Later, she saw Bob dancing with Beryl. Both were laughing and looked happy. Finding herself near Louella Dunn, Sally went to ask quietly if she felt all right.

'Not too tired?' Sally whispered, knowing how Louella Dunn hated being reminded of her invalid state.

Louella Dunn's eyes were bright. 'Not a bit tired, Sally. I'm so glad we've got that nice doctor on the island, aren't you? He always gave me a feeling of confidence...'

Sally nodded, unable to speak for a moment. She was watching Beryl and Bob dancing. What fun they were having, she thought—twisting, twirling, enjoying every moment of it.

She turned back to Louella Dunn. 'Should I slip up and see if your mother would like a glass of champagne?' Sally asked. 'I know they've dined but I could take her a few canapés which she loves and...'

Louella touched Sally's hand gently. 'It would be sweet of you. Mother likes to feel we remember her. You're looking very elegant tonight, Sally. Even Vincent said so.'

Sally's cheeks were hot. 'It's a beautiful gown. I don't know how to start thanking you...'

Louella touched her hand a second time. 'Then don't try, Sally. Money means nothing to us. It's not being generous unless it's a real sacrifice.' Her face clouded for a moment as if remembering her past. 'We love having you with us, Sally, and you must give us the pleasure of buying you things.'

'You know ... you know...' Against Sally's better judgement, the words tumbled out of her mouth. 'The rest is really doing you good, Mrs Dunn. Already you look different.'

Louella Dunn smiled. 'It's not the rest, Sally, it's ... it's Vincent,' she said, lowering her voice as Vincent danced past, in his arms the rather portly French woman who was smiling up at him.

'You know...' Sally said slowly, as if she was thinking aloud. 'He is a wonderful man...'

'It wouldn't be me you're after talking about, or would it, bechance?' Paddy asked, walking up quietly behind Sally, his brogue

122

exaggerated.

'Or me, the sea-faring doctor?' Bob asked, with a laugh.

Sally swung round. She had not heard the two men come up, so quietly had they walked. Beryl was standing there, too, a strange look on her face.

'She was talking about my husband,' Louella Dunn said, laughing. 'You two conceited creatures.'

'Your husband?' Paddy said gravely. 'Now there's a man for you. It's not fair at all, and that's the truth I'm saying. We haven't got a chance, Bob. Nary a chance when that man's around...'

Sally moved away quietly to go to the floor where the Esters lived. Why had Beryl looked at her so strangely as well as Bob? Both had seemed tense, as if annoyed about something.

Mrs Ester was sitting upright on a straight-backed chair, carefully darning a pair of Johnny's socks. She looked up at once, her face stiff with disapproval.

'Something wrong? I told Louella it was unwise...' she began.

Sally hurried to her. 'Your daughter sends her love and wondered if you'd like these canapés and a glass of champagne,' she said, turning to beckon the pretty Polynesian girl, who wore a red *pareu* and with a red flower behind one ear, and was carrying a tray, forward.

The girl gave a little bob and put the tray on a table by Mrs Ester's side, then hurried away. None of the servants liked the elderly woman for she had no patience with them and thought them lazy.

'That's very thoughtful of her,' Mrs Ester said slowly. 'Louella always was a thoughtful girl.'

'There's whisky for your husband,' Sally pointed out, 'and I brought him caviare.'

George Ester came in from the next room. He looked sleepy, his cheeks flushed as if he had just awakened from a nap. 'Did I hear the word "caviare"?' he asked. 'Good girl, Sally. Just what the doctor ordered.'

'Just what the doctor didn't order,' Mrs Ester said sharply.

George Ester ignored the remark. 'How's the party going, Sally? Everyone scrambling?' He chuckled. 'Vincent has quite a thing about that, hasn't he?'

'I think he's right, don't you?' Sally asked. 'I mean, it can be awful if you get stuck with a bore all the evening.'

Mrs Ester sniffed slightly. 'We were taught to suffer bores politely.'

'You were taught to be fools,' her husband said cheerfully. 'I agree with Sally. I like to wander—like the bee hovering over the flowers...' He began to chuckle but it ended in a choking, coughing fit.

'You see...' Mrs Ester said, her voice triumphant. 'I told you that you were smoking too much...'

Sally murmured an excuse and slipped away. She was so used to their perpetual arguments that she no longer noticed them. It was their son-in-law, Vincent Dunn, who had made her understand.

'They wouldn't say things like that if they really meant them, Sally. It's a sort of ritual people who've been married for a great many years fall into. A form of verbal lovemaking, in a way. In addition, Madre is actually worried about her husband's health but he gets impatient if she fusses, so she tries to get the message through this way,' Vincent Dunn had said.

As Sally slipped back into the big hall, Bob was waiting for her.

'Shall we dance?' he asked.

She could think of no excuse on the spur of the moment but wished she need not go into his arms. It was hard to dance properly, with this sweet breathlessness that yet had an acid taste for it meant nothing to him, and everything to her—even harder to talk.

'Was your kind action appreciated?' Bob asked.

Sally looked up. 'I think so,' she said stiffly.

'You like Mahane Island?' he asked. She nodded silently. 'Mr Dunn has kindly lent

125

me his car and chauffeur for the next week,' Bob went on. 'As I don't take up my duties until then, I wondered if you'd act as my guide?'

Sally's head jerked back sharply. 'Me?'

She saw the amusement in his eyes. 'Why not, you?'

Sally thought wildly. 'Well—well, you know I'm ... I mean, I'm employed and...'

'I spoke to Mr Dunn about it. He thought it an excellent idea,' Bob said, his voice grave, but his eyes bright. 'He said you were interested in local customs, as well. I may not have the same chance again, Sally, for I gather one doesn't get much time off at the hospital...'

Sally was thinking fast. She could hardly refuse to go without being asked for a reason. And how could she tell Bob and Mr Dunn the truth? That it was sheer agony to be with a man you love, when he doesn't even *see* you.

'Mrs Dunn might like to join us, Bob,' she began.

He was smiling. 'I've already asked her but she said no. The altitude tires her.'

It was like a slap in the face and it took Sally quite a few moments to recover. She was glad they were dancing so that she could keep her head down and Bob not see her expression.

So she was to go along as a guide. It was

126

not that Bob wanted her company. Quite the contrary. He wanted a guide and a chaperone, she told herself bitterly, or a guard?

'Perhaps Beryl...' she suggested tentatively.

'I'd rather not, if you don't mind,' Bob said. 'I want to see the island...'

The music stopped at that moment and he did not complete the sentence. He did not need to, Sally thought, as they walked towards Louella Dunn who was smiling at them. He had made it plain enough. He wanted to see the island—and if Beryl had gone along with them, it would have been only Beryl he could see.

CHAPTER SEVEN

Sally awoke to yet another perfect day. Cloudless blue sky, the ocean bright with the slanting darts of sunshine. Mahane Island was almost Paradise, she told herself. Occasionally one got squalls or a high wind, but nearly always the days were hot and the light breeze that usually sprang up in late afternoon made it even more pleasant.

She dressed with more than usual care, choosing a rather sophisticated, or so she hoped, green shantung frock. Bob always treated her as a child. She was not trying to attract him, she merely wanted to make a good impression.

She might as well have saved herself the trouble, she told herself later, as Bob came to the glass house in the car loaned by Vincent, together with Ruri, the Polynesian driver.

Bob gave Sally a quick look and grinned. 'My, we are growing up, Sally. You look quite twenty years and six months.'

To Sally's annoyance, her cheeks burned.

'Actually I am twenty years and seven months,' she said coldly.

'Who'd have thought it...' he said, taking her arm and leading her out into the bright sunshine and the huge red car that waited for them.

Sally's hands were shaking as she fumbled in her handbag for her dark glasses. Then she wished she hadn't opened her handbag for Bob was poking his finger in it, grinning like a Cheshire cat, she thought crossly.

'Everything but the kitchen sink, eh, Sally?' he said. 'You girls stagger me. Why do you have to carry so much stuff around?'

She could think of a dozen answers but decided to choose the simplest.

'Because we have to. Men have masses of pockets...'

He grinned again but this time, it was his friendly grin and Sally realized that as usual she was 'biting'.

128

She took a long deep breath. Why was she on this trip with Bob, she asked herself. Ruri was a better guide than she was. What was the idea? She had dreaded today and longed for it at the same time—which was ridiculous, inconsistent, and ... it just showed! She hadn't got over her love for Bob. Would she ever?

Now, sitting by his side in the car as it sped along the winding mountain road, she was very conscious of him. She stared ahead, keeping her voice formal as she pointed out different landmarks, or points of interest. She would not look at him! But she didn't need to for, had she been an artist, she told herself, she could have painted Bob's face perfectly. Those teasing green eyes—the mouth that would go all lop-sided in a smile, the red thick hair that rarely stayed smooth, the rather big nose, the unexpected freckles on his chin, the chin that was stubborn. Her love for him made her ache all over. Why had he come back, she asked herself miserably. And knew the answer.

'Slow up, Ruri, please...' Sally said, leaning forward to speak to the handsome Polynesian driver.

They stopped by a beautiful place just off the main road, where a waterfall tumbled down the mountainside to fall into a pool that sparkled in the sunshine. On the bank was a tiare tree, whose white satiny petals had a sweet but, to some, overwhelming scent. Sally thought the shiny green leaves reminded her of a gardenia.

'That flower is typical of Mahane Island,' Sally told Bob. 'When I smell that scent, I think of how happy the people are here, always singing and dancing, not worrying about the bomb or the future.'

As the car began to move, a pretty Polynesian girl sauntered along the road. The crimson flower in her long black hair matched the colour of her *pareu*. She walked lightly but her dark eyes were sultry and curious as she looked at Bob.

'Probably the first time she's seen a man with red hair,' Sally said.

Bob grinned. 'You don't say? Is it as attractive as all that?' he asked.

Sally gave him a quick look. 'Who said it was attractive?'

Walking by the girl, was an old woman, wearing a black Mother Hubbard.

'What a dress to wear on a hot day...' Bob commented.

'Paddy said that's a relic of a missionary,' Sally told him. 'When they—the missionaries, I mean—first came to the island they made the women wear these clothes.'

'Hideous,' Bob said.

The car stopped by the lagoon just as the fishermen were hauling in their nets and

Sally and Bob watched the women clapping their hands for joy as the fish poured out of the nets.

'I know it's silly,' Sally said, 'but I can't help feeling sorry for the fish.'

Bob looked at her oddly. 'Why not think of the hungry people to whom this will bring food and money?' he asked.

Sally's cheeks burned. It had been a stupid remark but need he be quite so cutting in his reply, she wondered. A huge white bird flew overhead, its tail feathers streaming behind.

'What sort of bird is that?' Bob asked.

'Paddy says it's a tropic bird...' Sally said. They watched the powerful bird as it swooped and rose again on the air currents.

'Paddy seems to know a lot,' Bob said, his voice noncommittal.

Sally gave him a quick glance. 'He's travelled a lot.'

'I can imagine,' Bob said, his tone changing, becoming slightly sarcastic.

Ruri stopped the car by the reef. The high seas were racing in, there was a wind blowing and the cloud of spray enveloped them, stinging Sally's cheeks, making both Sally and Bob laugh and duck and tell a grinning Ruri to drive on.

'The *maraamu* has started. That's a cold wind that blows for about a week every month. Mrs Ester loathes it but I find it refreshing,' Sally said.

The car passed a group of dancers, pretty laughing girls whose skirts swung provocatively as they danced to the music of a guitar.

'Do the men dance?' Bob asked, leaning back, folding his arms, his face oddly stiff.

Sally laughed. 'And how! They wear grass skirts over their *pareus*, you see. I haven't seen much dancing yet but Paddy says it's out of this world. Terrifically exciting, he says. The rhythm is fabulous and makes you almost drunk, he told me once. His blood begins to boil and he wants to join in.'

'How absurd he would look,' Bob said lightly, his face still stiff.

Sally gave him a quick glance. 'I believe he's a fine dancer. I know we once had Scottish dancing in honour of one of Mr Dunn's Scottish guests and Paddy led us...'

'He appears to be a man of many parts...' Bob commented. He leaned forward and pointed to two Polynesian men, walking on the narrow path at the edge of the road. They had poles on their shoulders, balanced, carrying double loads. 'What have they got there?'

'Probably taro root, papaya and bread fruit,' Sally told him.

'What sort of food do they live on?'

'Fish and *poi*, and modern food nowadays but Paddy says that's not a good thing. They like food out of tins too much and it's too

132

expensive. Tahitian meals can be wonderful, Bob ... We had to attend a feast, once, and it was incredible the amount of food we had ... Cubed raw fish in coconut sauce...' Her laugh rang out. 'Luckily I didn't know what it was and enjoyed it. Poor Mrs Ester had a piece in her mouth when Paddy explained that it was raw fish, soaked in lime juice and then in coconut sauce. I told Paddy it was mean of him but he's always playing tricks like that. We had sucking pig, too. They wrap it in leaves and it is left for hours in a ground oven. It tastes delicious.'

The car was spinning along the level road, taking them past the office buildings, the wharf where a schooner was in, being unloaded, past Polynesians riding bicycles or sauntering along, often singing, or twanging a guitar.

'It's a colourful place,' Bob said slowly. 'You seem very happy, here.'

'Oh, I am...' Sally said fervently. 'Everyone's so nice and friendly.'

'You get on well with ... with Mr Dunn?' Bob asked casually.

Sally turned to look at him, her hand brushing her hair back. 'Oh, I do. He's a marvellous person, Bob. So patient and understanding. He's taught me so much...'

'I can imagine,' Bob's voice was dry.

Sally was puzzled but went on: 'He taught me poise and how to meet people. Working

133

for him is fun for he gives one a lot of praise—but it isn't easy, in a way. He expects perfection.'

'Mrs Dunn is looking better...' Bob began.

'Yes, isn't she?' Sally twisted herself round to look at a laughing Polynesian girl on the side of the road, her hair swinging forward over her face, as she pulled a little child along on a palm leaf. The little boy was laughing and shouting. 'I love them,' Sally said impulsively. 'They're all so happy.'

'How would you define happiness, Sally?' Bob asked.

She was startled, her hand going to her mouth as it often did when she was nervous.

'Define...?'

He nodded. 'What makes you happy, for instance? What do you need to be happy, shall we say?' he asked.

Sally stared at him, feeling her cheeks grow hot, looking away quickly lest he read the truth in her eyes. What made her happy, she asked herself. Had she ever been so really happy as in that moment when she had stood in his arms, his mouth warm on hers, her whole body tingling with the wonder of it? She wondered what he would say if she told him the truth. Angry? Embarrassed? Impatient with her for making something out of a casual kiss?

'I don't know...' she said, aware that she

was lying. 'I like being with certain people, having lots of sunshine, not too much work to do...'

'Being with Paddy Masters, for instance?' Bob asked.

Her cheeks were really burning now but luckily she could be angry which helped her compose herself. She looked at the man sitting by her side.

'Is there something wrong in liking Paddy?' she asked indignantly. 'You're always getting little digs at him. Why don't you like him?'

Bob frowned. 'Honestly, Sally, you do jump to conclusions. How can I like a man I have met only a couple of times? Maybe I'm getting rather tired of his name. Every other word you say is "Paddy".'

Sally caught her breath. 'It is not...'

'It is. Now go on talking but watch yourself. I'll count the number of times you mention Paddy Masters in the next five minutes. I think you'll be surprised,' Bob said.

Sally stared at the big white building on the side of the road that they were approaching.

'That's a surprisingly big hospital...' she began and caught herself just in time. She had nearly added that Paddy had told her about the first few weeks when there was no doctor or hospital on the island and two of

135

the staff had been very ill.

'Yes, very well staffed,' Bob said. 'I like Matron especially. Efficient yet human. I think we shall get on very well.'

'The doctor that's going? Why is he going, do you know?'

'I think he's going back to England to get married. His fiancée doesn't like the idea of living on a tropical island so far from civilisation,' Bob told her.

Sally turned to look at him. 'But it's his life ... his career. Paddy...' She stopped herself just too late.

Bob grinned and held up one finger.

Sally swung round to stare ahead. It was absurd. She wasn't always talking about Paddy. It was just that Paddy had taught her all she knew of the islanders and so she often quoted him.

'I wonder if Ruri could take us to the school,' Bob asked casually.

Sally felt herself stiffen. Beryl would be at the school. Was that perhaps the reason Bob disliked Paddy? Because he was jealous and hated the thought of Beryl working with Paddy? The familiar aching pain filled her and it was hard to talk lightly.

'Of course. Paddy...' She stopped but again, it was too late. 'He likes visitors,' she went on lamely, conscious that Bob must be grinning, and holding up another finger.

'What sort of people are the islanders?'

136

Bob asked as the car turned at a cross-roads and began to climb a long leisurely slope up the side of the mountain.

'They ... I think ... I was told...' Sally began, trying to find a way of avoiding Paddy's name.

Bob burst out laughing. 'Skip it, Sally. The strain is showing on your face,' he said. 'Paddy says ... You take over from there...'

Sally felt her cheeks hot. 'Paddy says that they are capricious but that we must accept this trait in them. They get bored easily with what they're doing ... it's ... it's called *fiu*. They just walk out on the job whether they've finished it or not, but then they come back in a few days or a few months to finish it. I like them. Always singing and laughing and, our staff, at any rate, are very good tempered. Why?'

'I was wondering what sort of patients they'll make,' Bob said.

'That's the school,' Sally told him, pointing to a large thatched house with open sides, built up on stilts above the ground. Sally could see the children sitting at their desks and Paddy at the blackboard. She and Bob climbed the wide ladder that led to the school and Paddy came to meet them. His hair was brushed smooth but a few wisps still defied discipline.

'And it's visitors we're having...' he said. 'Welcome, Doctor ... and Sally. Come inside...'

Sally had been to the school before but it was all new to Bob and Paddy showed him round and introduced 'the new doctor and mind you do as he says' to the boys and girls of various ages who formed the school.

Beryl was sitting with a group of pre-school age children and she stood up eagerly.

'Hi ... Bob...' she said.

Bob grinned. 'Hi. Am I too old to join the class?' he asked.

Sally closed her eyes for a moment. You had only to see the way Bob looked at Beryl...

'I'm afraid so,' Beryl said. She wore a simple yellow frock, her long black hair loosely tied in a pony-tail. Her face was flushed, her eyes bright as she came to talk to Bob. 'I never thought I'd be teaching children—or anyone,' she confessed.

Bob smiled. 'Enjoying it?' he asked.

Beryl gave a quick glance at Sally. 'Loving it,' Beryl said.

Sally was trying not to listen in to their conversation, but the big airy room was quiet as the children sat back, watching them. Paddy was showing Sally a painting Johnny had done, asking her what she thought of it.

'It's a tiki...' Johnny explained carefully.

Sally stared at the painting that was bold in outlines as well as colour. It was of a square-looking statue of a man, arms folded. Hewn out of stone, there were deep holes for his eyes and mouth.

'What's a tiki, Johnny?' Bob asked, moving to her side.

Johnny opened his mouth and then, with a quick look at Paddy, closed it again.

Paddy was looking at Sally. 'Are you showing the doctor the island?' he asked.

Sally nodded. 'Yes, Mr Dunn thought it a good chance before Bob started work.'

Bob was startled at the jealousy that swept through him. Was it really necessary for Sally to explain why she was with him? Was he wrong about Vincent Dunn? Was it Paddy Masters with whom Sally was in love? Look at their conversation on the drive! Paddy this, Paddy that, until Bob had wanted to scream. And now, Bob was thinking, look at the expression on Paddy's face—and the quick way Sally had justified her reason for being with the new doctor.

Bob looked round the big airy room. It was a good school, he could see that. The children looked interested in their work. Johnny, he had been told, had blossomed in his new environment, enjoying his work, eager to get on. That added up—to the fact that Paddy Masters was an excellent teacher but . . .

Bob caught himself frowning, annoyed with himself. Sally had accused him of disliking Paddy. Bob was shocked to find that she was right. He did dislike this pseudo-Irishman, half-bum, half-good type. Bob was shocked at the anger that was flooding him as he saw the way Paddy put his arm lightly round Sally's shoulder and spoke.

'I suggest you take along our young student, Sally. Johnny can show you the tikis and tell you a lot of island lore.' Paddy was smiling at the small boy. 'Like to do that, Johnny? Then write a composition on what you showed them as your homework?'

Johnny's cheeks were flushed. 'Oh, thanks, Paddy, I mean, sir. I'll not be a moment, Sally...' He darted behind a tall reed screen and returned in a moment with his satchel, stuffing an exercise book in it.

'I'm ready,' he announced.

Bob was annoyed. He had no desire to be given a lecture by a ten-year-old boy on 'tikis', whatever they were. He wasn't interested. He wanted to see the island, not tikis—and he wanted Sally's companionship. He still was not sure why he had asked Vincent Dunn if he might take Sally with him on his tour of Mahane Island, even less sure why he had wanted to be alone with her. Yet the urge to be with her, to see for himself if he was right and she was in love with Vincent Dunn—even though she might not know it herself—had been too strong for him. Yet what had he learned? He and Sally had seemed to fight all the time—she had talked of no one but Paddy and now Bob admitted to himself, he was more puzzled than ever.

One thing stood out, though. Paddy was as jealous as he was. Whatever Sally felt about Paddy, Bob was certain that Paddy was in love with Sally. Look at the way Sally had explained why she was with Bob! And at how Paddy had organized things so that they should no longer be alone. What a...

Bob caught himself having to swallow the anger that rose in him, catching him in the throat, threatening to explode. Then as he calmed down, Bob thought with dismay of what a fool he was. He had always prided himself on being a well-balanced man—yet now he was acting like a crazy, lovelorn fool! So long as no one had noticed, he thought worriedly.

'Fine, Johnny,' Bob said with an artificial cheerfulness. 'Just what we need to help us understand the island. Thanks,' Bob looked at Paddy with a wry smile, 'for loaning us such a good guide.'

Johnny was in fine fettle in the car, directing the driver, taking them as close as the car would go to the things he had to show them. Johnny's young face was earnest as he talked.

'You see, even Ruri is scared,' Johnny

said, lowering his voice. 'All the islanders are. I think it's rather daft...' he added scornfully. 'I mean, a tiki isn't anything alive—it's just a stone god. Awfully ugly, too. He always keeps his hands on his chest and he never smiles. There are lots in the jungle and the old *mareas*, too. That's a temple, Dr Chart...' Johnny said, looking up at Bob who was trying to appear interested.

Sally was sitting very still, gazing out of the window at the palm trees waving in the breeze and at the lagoons far below them.

'They're also scared of *tupapaus*, doctor,' Johnny said.

Bob heard Johnny's voice from afar; he was trying to will Sally to turn and look at him—perhaps then her eyes would betray the truth, and he would know if she loved Paddy Masters.

'D'you know what a *tupapau* is, doctor?' Johnny insisted, tugging at Bob's arm.

Bob looked down and felt ashamed. Johnny was only trying to instruct him in the island lore and here he was, Bob thought, behaving like an ill-mannered moron.

'No, I don't, Johnny. What is it?' Bob asked.

'It's a sort of ghost, only not a nasty one. It's like a ... lep...'

'Leprechaun, Johnny,' Sally supplied the word gently.

Trust her to know that, Bob was thinking

142

crossly. Anything to do with that irritating Irishman, Sally would know!

'That's right,' Johnny was saying. 'You see, doctor, the islanders don't think we go to heaven when we die. They think we stay here for hundreds of years, keeping an eye on our de … de …'

'Descendants?' Bob said quickly, before Sally could.

Johnny nodded. 'Yes, and we become *tupapaus*. They don't always hurt people, sometimes they just tease them. Sometimes, though, they do kill you. I think it's rather stupid to be scared of them, don't you?'

Bob looked thoughtful. 'I suppose we're just as superstitious, I mean, not wanting to walk under ladders…'

'But that's different. That's in case someone drops paint on you,' Johnny said scornfully. 'I'm not scared of *tupapaus*. They say if you spit at them or grab a stick and make a sort of swishing noise, you can scare the *tupapau* away. One day, I'll show the others that I'm not scared of anything…' Johnny added proudly.

'I'm sure you're not, Johnny,' Bob said. 'Are you learning the language?'

'Gosh, I most certainly am, doctor,' Johnny said. '*Aita peopea* … that's the most important thing to know, Mr Masters says. It means it doesn't matter. Nothing really matters because it can always be put right or

143

done another day.'

'Quite a comforting philosophy,' Bob said dryly, glancing at the silent girl by their side. But Sally did not seem to hear him, she was gazing across at a small atoll out in the blue sea.

She was feeling miserable, the old ache returning to taunt her. How quickly Bob had leapt at the chance to have Johnny along with them. Look at him, now, talking to Johnny, interested in all the small boy had to say, completely ignoring Sally.

Sally closed her eyes, unable for once to enjoy the green beauty of the island with its tall palm trees, so graciously graceful, tropical flowers in their bright colours, red, yellow, purple, the glimpses of silvery waterfalls, the floating lilies in the pools and always the faint intoxicating scent of flowers, the sound of music and laughter.

Why had Bob come back, she asked herself for the millionth time. And, for the millionth time, knew the answer.

Because he loved Beryl.

CHAPTER EIGHT

As Louella Dunn's 'Independence Day', as she called it, approached, Louella grew more and more impatient.

144

'If only the days didn't drag so,' she said to Sally as they sat on the terrace, looking over towards the ocean.

The evening before there had been heavy rains and winds but now everything had a clean, newly-washed look and the air was pleasant to the skin.

'Not much longer,' Sally said comfortingly.

Mrs Ester looked up from her large wicker chair and laid down her mending for a moment.

'If you did some sewing, Louella, you wouldn't be so bored!' she began.

'I loathe sewing,' her daughter said frankly, and then smiled. ''Sides, if I did the mending, Mother, what would you do?'

Mrs Ester sighed. 'How long are we staying on this deserted island, Louella? Has Vincent given you any idea?' She waved her hand in a strangely theatrical manner. 'All this money spent and for how long? A year or two, at the most.'

'But the house will be sold, Mother,' Louella said patiently. 'Vincent has already been offered a fabulous sum for it. They'll make it into an hotel and then...'

'Why doesn't he take the offer?' Mrs Ester asked. 'They may change their minds later...'

'But Vincent's work here isn't finished...' Louella began. With a murmured excuse,

Sally left them.

She hurried upstairs to her bedroom, the luxury of which still amazed her. Standing by the window, she could see some yachts going out through the opening in the reef.

Was Bob in one of them, Sally wondered. She rested her face against the cool glass and watched the way the yachts sped along so gracefully, their coloured spinnakers billowing in the wind.

Since Bob had taken over the job at the hospital, she had seen little of him. Of course, he occasionally came to dinner, or they would meet at one of the club dances, but she had never been alone with him since that drive round the island.

She went to the dressing-table and looked at her reflection in the long mirror. Surely she looked older and more sophisticated, she thought. She picked up the hair-brush and began to rhythmically brush her straight hair.

Bob was doing a lot of sailing so he was probably happy, she thought. He had taken Beryl out several times but poor Beryl had come back, looking green and confessing that she had not enjoyed it much. But Bob had not asked her, Sally thought, the brush moving firmly through her hair. Not that she would have gone if he had asked her, she told herself hastily, and knew it was a lie.

It was awful to live so near and yet so far from someone you could not stop loving.

She was careful never to mention his name and yet, at times, she wondered if that was wise. But she was particularly careful where Paddy Masters was concerned. Paddy had a knack of reading her thoughts and although he had never said anything, yet several times she had caught him looking at her oddly when Bob's name had come into the conversation.

Sally put down the hairbrush. She felt restless and unsettled. She curled up on the foot of the bed and took the varnish off her nails. This was one of her slack days. Mr Dunn and Rosalie had gone over to Papeete on business. There would be no guests that evening so they could all relax.

Waving one hand in the air to dry the fresh varnish she had applied, Sally thought over the conversation on the terrace. The weeks had grown into months and soon Mrs Dunn's six months rest would be over and she could lead a normal life. What would happen, then, Sally wondered. In the past months, there had been many bad moments when Mrs Ester had started to interfere and by deftly forestalling her, Vincent Dunn had postponed the bad moment. But could he still do that when his wife was up and about?

'The moment of no return,' he had called it once to Sally. 'My mother-in-law and I must never quarrel,' he had continued. 'For that will be the moment of no return. She'll leave here and Louella will never be able to forgive me.'

The nails of both hands finished, Sally looked at them thoughtfully. Mrs Ester was a difficult woman. Nothing seemed to please. She grumbled if there were guests staying overnight, said the the house was noisy. She grumbled if there were no guests and said they led a static existence, like cabbages. She grumbled if Johnny was too lively, and worried if he was too quiet.

Today, for instance. Mr Dunn had asked both the Esters if they would like to go to Papeete with him. George Ester had been keen to accept but his wife had said no, very firmly. George had been slightly off colour for a few days and Mrs Ester had said the journey would be too tiring and she didn't want to go. Yet less than an hour later, she had called it a 'deserted island'.

If Mrs Ester was getting restless, it was a bad sign and maybe Mr Dunn should be warned. It made it worse that Mrs Dunn felt the same *malade* as Rosalie always called it.

The door opened abruptly and Mrs Cameron, the American housekeeper, stood there. A big buxom woman who seldom spoke and never smiled, yet was always friendly in a distant manner, she came, as usual, straight to the point.

'Will you drive one of the garden boys to the hospital, Sally?' she said. 'There's been a couple of ugly accidents. Fighting. I've put a tourniquet on his arm but the sooner we get him to the doctor the better. You can drive?'

Sally was on her feet. 'Of course.'

Which was near the truth, if not the whole truth. Rosalie had given her several lessons and Sally drove quite a lot round the island, but whether she could drive through traffic, was another matter. Not that there was any need to worry, she told herself, as she hurried down to the hall where the car keys were always kept. There was little traffic on the island.

She found the patient in the little Mini she used. Mrs Cameron was waiting, her face concerned.

'I've got a couple more here to see to but they're not urgent. Just tell the doctor about them.'

Sally looked at the man slumped in the seat. His shirt sleeve was ugly with blood, the wound hidden by a blood-stained bandage. His eyes were closed and his face badly cut and still bleeding. Mrs Cameron showed Sally the tourniquet, giving her instructions how often it must be loosened before being re-tightened.

'You've got a watch on you?' she asked crisply.

Sally swallowed. 'Yes.' It would take her a good twenty-five minutes to get to the hospital. Supposing she did the wrong thing?

149

Forgot...?

Mrs Cameron turned away. 'I think he'll be all right—they're pretty tough...' she said.

Sally started the car and slid the gear into place. She felt nervous but told herself that was ridiculous. After all, Mrs Cameron had told her the man would be all right.

Driving along the road, every now and then looking worriedly at her watch, Sally kept glancing down at the unconscious man by her side. Her hands were shaking a little as she carried out Mrs Cameron's instructions, stopped the car and released the tourniquet and then tightened it. Swinging round a sharp turn in the road, a car coming from the opposite direction had to swerve to avoid her. Sally knew she was in the right for the other car had been on the wrong side of the road but it set her heart pounding madly and her cheeks were red-hot by the time she stopped outside the hospital.

She almost tumbled out of the car and hurried inside. A tall, red-headed man in a green robe with a matching cap tipped back on his head and his mask hanging below his chin, paused as he saw her.

'Sally—' His voice was sharp. 'What's wrong?'

She grabbed his arm without realizing it as the words poured out of her mouth.

'Mrs Cameron says it was a fight—a badly

150

injured arm. There's a tourniquet...'

He stared at her for a moment and then gently but firmly, removed her hands and strode outside, his cumbersome theatre boots slowing him up. Sally was close behind.

'I did loosen it, Bob...' she was saying. 'There are two more hurt but Mrs Cameron said not to worry so long as you come down later...'

She wondered if he had heard her for as he leaned over the unconscious man, he seemed to change and become a different person. In a few moments, he had two orderlies with a stretcher outside the hospital and they were lifting the wounded man out of the car, taking him inside.

In a small but immaculately clean surgery, Bob carefully undid the bandage. Sally, standing nearby, felt suddenly sick as she saw the depth and size of the wound, the gleam of white bone through the parted flesh.

'I'll have to operate...' Bob was saying briskly, striding away, leaving Sally to wonder what she should do next.

She hovered in the lofty cool hall. Had Bob understood that Mrs Cameron wanted him to come and see the other patients later? Should she wait and tell him or...

A very pretty blonde nurse came and asked her what she wanted. She was new on the island and seemed glad to find someone to talk to.

'I never thought it would be as quiet as this,' she confessed, 'but I guess I'll stay...' She smiled as Sally asked why.

The nurse chuckled and at that moment, both saw Bob striding across the other end of the hall, Matron bustling along behind him as he spoke rapidly over his shoulder.

'That's why,' the nurse told Sally. 'Boy, he's smooth. Don't you think?'

Sally hesitated. 'Yes, he's ... he's all right.'

The nurse looked at her as if she was out of her mind.

'The understatement of the year,' she said with a laugh. 'That red hair just slays me. Now...' She became briskly professional. 'What can I do for you?'

Sally told her how she had brought the wounded man to the hospital, about Mrs Cameron's request that the doctor come down to see two others when he was free.

'I did tell him but I don't think he was listening,' Sally said and felt herself blushing at the way the nurse looked at her.

'Dr Chart misses nothing, you can take my word for that,' the nurse was saying. 'All the same, I'll remind him when he comes out of the theatre.'

'Thanks...' Sally said and left the building.

Driving home slowly, she thought how

different Bob had looked in the hospital from how he had looked on the ship. Here he looked as if he was part of the hospital—it was the right sort of background for him. She would imagine he was a good conscientious doctor. If only...

She deliberately blocked her thoughts. She would not think about Bob Chart, she told herself firmly. She'd think instead of Paddy Masters.

She drove round the steep corner carefully but met no one this time, She fidgeted a little in her seat, getting comfortable, beginning to relax.

Now Paddy was a really nice man, she told herself. And yet ... sometimes, she got annoyed with him. His jokes often misfired. Like Johnny, Sally had decided to learn the language of the islands. Paddy had offered to teach her but she had grown a little suspicious after a while, for when she tried out the phrases Paddy had taught her, the Polynesians had doubled up with laughter and so she had known that Paddy had been playing a trick on her.

She was on the last strip of road towards the glass house, now. Yet Paddy, she told herself, would never willingly or intentionally hurt anyone. Could she say the same about Bob, she wondered. He knew how she hated being treated as someone very young and naive, yet persisted in treating her like that.

That wasn't very kind. On the other hand, if she was really sophisticated, wouldn't his teasing merely amuse her?

She parked the car, took the keys inside, and then went in search of Mrs Cameron to tell her what happened.

Mrs Cameron was busy. She had two garden boys, sitting on a bench, both being bandaged and looking very sorry for themselves.

'I don't think I'll need the doctor,' she told Sally.

Sally tried to hide her dismay. 'I told him but I'll ring up the hospital...'

'Don't bother,' Mrs Cameron said. 'I will. I want to find out how Tarupau is...'

It was two hours later that Sally, softly playing the grand piano in the lounge, heard Bob's voice.

'But I was distinctly told...' he was saying angrily.

Sally hurried to the hall. Bob was talking to Beryl, his face annoyed. He looked up and saw Sally.

'I thought you said Mrs Cameron wanted me to see her other casualties...' he said crossly. 'I've rushed down here and now Beryl says they're all right...'

'Mrs Cameron did ask me to tell you,' Sally told him. 'Then when I got back, she said they didn't need you...'

'Surely the least you could have done was

154

to let me know,' Bob said crossly, turning away. 'I'm up to my eyes in troubles, as it is...'

'Mrs Cameron said she'd...' Sally began but Bob had gone, striding out of the house.

Sally and Beryl stared at one another as they heard the car start up, heard the impatient revving of the engine and then the roar as the car leapt forward.

'He is in a rage,' Beryl said, smiling a little.

'It wasn't my fault...' Sally said.

Beryl gave her an odd look. 'But he thinks it was...' she said and turned away.

Sally went back to the piano, letting her fingers rest lightly on the keys. All desire to play had left her. Surely Bob could have given her the chance to explain? After all, she thought, it hadn't been her fault but ... But as Beryl had said, Bob thought it was!

Quietly Sally played as she thought. What was the matter with Beryl these days? Moody and unfriendly towards Sally. Why? And why was she always so off-handed with Paddy? If Paddy spoke to Beryl, Beryl barely had the grace to answer him, and if she did, it was always a curt reply. It was odd how those two seemed to dislike one another, Sally thought.

She stood up, quietly closing the lid of the piano. She would go for a walk round the garden. She did wish Bob had given her a chance to explain, she thought. Should she 'phone him and tell him that Mrs Cameron had promised to let him know? And if she did that, what would he think, she wondered. Would he believe her? And if he did, would he accuse her of giving Mrs Cameron away and say that probably Mrs Cameron had been too busy to 'phone him?' Whatever she did with Bob, seemed to be wrong, Sally thought unhappily, as she walked over the lovely, smooth grass, admired the perfectly designed beds and then stood, gazing at the ocean before her.

The familiar ache of misery swept through her. Maybe it would be best if she handed in her notice and went back to London. Mr Dunn would understand. Soon, his wife would be able to help him more fully with his entertaining so they would not miss her, Sally thought. Wouldn't it be easier to get over this hopeless loving if she was thousands of miles away?

*   *   *

When, two days later. Bob received an invitation from Vincent Dunn to join the family in a yachting trip, he hesitated about accepting it. He was still in a state of fury at Sally's casual behaviour. When he had seen her in the hospital hall, her cheeks ablaze, her chest rising and falling rapidly, and she had grabbed at his arm as if for support, he had been frightened for her. He had thought in that instant of a million things. Had she been bitten by a snake? Had she fallen...

And the relief when he heard that she was not the one in trouble, had been breathtaking. It had shocked him—the complete withdrawal of fear that had drained away, leaving him almost empty. He had become very crisp and professional in case she noticed. He had noted what she said about the other casualties, had lost himself in the need for caring for the injured man and it had only been after the op. was successfully over and he was stripping himself of his gown and cap and mask, tossing the gloves away and washing up, that he remembered the wave of fear he had felt for Sally. It was then that the new little nurse who seemed to haunt his every movement, had sidled up to him with the message from Sally.

'She seemed scared in case you forgot, Doctor,' the blonde girl had said, her dark blue eyes predatory. 'But I said you never forgot anything.'

He'd grinned. 'I see. Like an elephant,' he had said and had been amused at her dismay.

'Oh, Doctor, I didn't mean that. Really I didn't...' she was saying, still running after him as he made his way to the Matron's office.

He had a hard day's work ahead of him. An epidemic of enteritis, a suspected case of typhoid, the mysterious illness of a baby, an expected delivery at any moment ... but maybe it would be wise to slip down to the Dunns house and see what was up. He had felt it must be pretty serious for Sally to have given the blonde little nurse a message after she had already told him.

He had walked in the house to find Beryl in the hall.

'The fight the garden boys had?' she had asked and laughed. 'They're fine. Mrs Cameron saw to that.'

It had been then that his anger had flared up and when Sally had tried to excuse herself, he had remembered the fear he had felt for her, and oddly enough, it had made him as angry with himself as he was with her. So angry, indeed, that he had feared what he might say and had taken refuge in retreat. Had driven back to the hospital in a raging temper and was still in it, he told himself.

He turned over the neatly-typed invitation. He wondered who had typed it. Sally? Rosalie? One of her staff?

He knew Vincent Dunn had a very fine yacht but rarely used it. Bob had often wondered if Dunn owned it as a status symbol. Bob had learned enough since he came to the island to know that Dunn had fingers in many pies and that his basic need was to appear and act as a very wealthy man.

Bob Chart walked to the window of his

surgery. The ocean with its great waves called to him, tempted him. Could he, without worry, leave the hospital? How long would they be away?

On an instinct, he 'phoned what Sally called the 'glass house'. To his surprise, Sally answered.

Bluntly he told her what he wanted to know. 'I don't know if I can leave the hospital. How long'll we be out in the yacht?'

Sally hesitated. 'Not more than three hours,' she said and he wondered why her voice was stiff. 'Mr Dunn wants to give his wife and Mrs Ester a change of locale ... It seems both are feeling restless and not very happy.'

'It seems?' Bob echoed.

Sally hesitated again. 'Actually it was my idea, Bob. Mrs Ester said this was a deserted island and Mrs Dunn said the days drag. I thought it might help to pass the time...'

'Pass the time...' he said sarcastically. 'I only wish I could get some time.'

'Life's hard at the hospital?' Sally asked, her voice more friendly.

'Life's always hard in any hospital,' Bob told her.

'It might also be hard on a ship,' Sally said quietly.

Bob stood very still, holding his breath. 'You don't approve of my dream,' he said accusingly.

159

He heard Sally catch her breath. 'No, I didn't mean that, Bob. I merely meant that ... that one can imagine that what one isn't doing would always be easier...'

'It all sounds rather involved,' he said dryly. 'D'you imagine anything you could do could possibly be easier than what you are doing now?'

Again she caught her breath and he could hear it. 'In a way, I do,' she said and rang off.

He stood still for a while, tempted to ring again, but sure she would manage not to answer it. What had she meant—'in a way, I do'? What could be easier than her present life? High salary, luxurious surroundings, practically no work, her beloved Paddy Masters...

Could she have meant that she was unhappy? Had she, he thought, discovered that she was in love with Vincent Dunn and could that be tearing her apart? Knowing Sally as he did, he felt sure that the mere idea of being in love with a married man—and most of all a man married to Louella, whom she admired and to whom she owed so much—would be terrifying.

He decided to go on the trip and scribbled a hasty note accepting and thanking Vincent Dunn for the invitation for the next day.

The yacht, *Miranda*, was a bigger one than Bob had expected and when he parked the hospital car on the wharf and went aboard, he looked round curiously.

Dunn knew what he was doing, Bob decided. The boat was in excellent condition, the crew well-trained and alert. It was a beautiful as well as comfortable craft. Bob envied Dunn the wealth that had bought it. How long would he have to save before he and Soar could build a boat even half this size?

Bob was one of the first on board and he relaxed in a chair as the hustle and bustle of an out-going craft went on around him. He leapt to his feet as he saw the Dunns coming. Vincent was pushing his wife's wheel-chair, the Esters were close behind, Johnny was talking to Sally and...

'No Beryl?' Bob asked after he had greeted them.

Mrs Dunn laughed. 'Poor darling, you know she's always seasick so there's no point in her coming along.'

After the older folk were settled in comfortable chairs, Bob found himself next to Sally as they leaned on the rail.

'Where's the Irishman?' Bob asked.

Sally glanced at him. 'I don't know. He doesn't go in for sailing.'

'Do you?'

She hesitated. 'I don't know. This is my first time.'

They were casting the moorings, now. For a moment, Bob forgot his companion and watched the deft, well-trained movements of the crew. The sails were still furled but the powerful motor was soon running smoothly as the graceful craft set off towards the opening in the reef.

When Bob turned to speak to Sally again, she had gone. Johnny was in her place.

'You're a sailor, Doctor, aren't you?' Johnny asked eagerly. 'Would you brief me, please, sir? I've got to write a composition about this for homework and I don't know the names of anything.'

'Will Mr Masters?' Bob asked and then was ashamed of his sarcasm.

Johnny's young eyes were clear and innocent. 'Mr Masters knows everything,' he said firmly.

'I see,' Bob said with a rueful grin. 'Well, first of all, Johnny...' he began.

*   *   *

Sally was leaning against the railing, her body braced, her straight blonde hair blowing in her eyes as the boat went through the opening and met the ocean waves. With a roaring sound, the sails reared, turning from a shapeless mass of white cotton and becoming things of beauty as they billowed in the strong wind. Sally had been somewhat scared lest she be a bad sailor but as the yacht dipped and rose, and rode the powerful waves, she found her body responding to every movement, and knew that she was blessed—she was a good sailor.

Bob was talking to Johnny, who seemed to be hanging on every word, Sally noticed. How quickly Bob had ignored her, his attention caught so easily by the movements of the sailors. This was the life he wanted—to live like this, to eat, sleep and work on a yacht. As she braced her legs apart and let her body go with the movement, she caught some of the magic that Bob must love. She looked up at the great sails and loved the sound of the wind in them. It was fascinating—it was like flying but somehow much more personal. Here you were part of the boat—in an airplane, you were a thing apart.

She glanced at the Dunns. Louella's cheeks were flushed, her eyes happy as she talked to her husband who was now at the wheel. The Esters were sitting together, George smoking happily, the wind blowing the smoke into his wife's face. Mrs Ester's eyes were closed, her mouth a pursed button of distaste, but her hands were relaxed on her lap and Sally had a strange feeling that Mrs Ester was enjoying the trip far more than she would ever admit.

Sally was really sorry when it was time for them to go home. As the craft sped through the water before the wind, the sails roaring,

Sally drew in deep long breaths of air. She had stood alone at the rail for the whole of the voyage, just loving every moment of it. Perhaps for the first time, she understood how Bob felt, she thought. How exciting to go round the world on a yacht like this. She had been below—the cabins were small but beautifully furnished and planned. The galley would be fun to cook in...

Her thoughts skidded to a standstill. Bob had said that sailing round the world was not for women, she remembered. He had been very firm about it, even sarcastic. No matter who Bob married, he would leave her behind. But then, hadn't she forgotten, she asked herself, Bob had said he wasn't going to get married? He called it a 'trap'. Had he changed his mind because of Beryl, Sally wondered. Yet they were rarely alone together, nor did he call at the house to see her. Perhaps Bob was fighting his love for Beryl, she thought. After all, his first words when they came on board had been:

'No Beryl?'

Wasn't that proof enough?

CHAPTER NINE

There was an argument about Louella Dunn's 'return to normal living', as she called it. Although not really surprised at Mrs Ester's reaction, Sally found herself feeling cross with her, for she kept insisting that her daughter should return to normal living only 'by degrees'.

'You're bound to be weak after being in bed so long,' Mrs Ester declared.

They were sitting on the terrace, enjoying the shade of the huge striped umbrellas, sipping ice-cold drinks.

'Oh, Mother...' Louella Dunn protested, waving a leaf fan before her face, her eyes unhappy. 'I'm not weak. I've been able to walk to the bathroom every day...'

'I still think...' Mrs Ester began, her cheeks flushed from heat and annoyance.

Sally bit her lip, fighting back the words she longed to say. Sometimes she failed completely to understand Mrs Ester; sometimes, she wondered if she ever had understood her. One moment, Mrs Ester was urging her daughter to be a real wife to Vincent, to share his interests, his life, to be a 'partner and not a passenger,' as she had put it; the next moment, Mrs Ester was trying to imply that Louella was delicate and must always be pampered.

Vincent Dunn stood up suddenly, stubbing out his cigarette, smiling at his mother-in-law stiffly.

'I agree with you, Madre, but I don't want to spoil Louella's happiness. She's looked

165

forward to tomorrow so much. I suggest we seek medical advice. I'll ring young Chart and see if he can come down and lunch with us...'

Before anyone could answer him, he had left them, walking across the tiled terrace, his shoulders braced so that Sally knew how angry he was, and how hard he was trying to fight it.

'I think you should get up for an hour a day at first,' Mrs Ester went on. 'I know what will happen. Louella. You'll be so excited that you'll start your headaches, again. You'll be back where you started...'

Sally made her escape as soon as she could. No wonder poor Mrs Dunn was always having headaches, if this was the way her mother always behaved.

She met Vincent Dunn in the hall and he smiled ruefully.

'Did it show, Sally?' he asked. 'I'm afraid my armour is wearing very thin.'

'I thought you handled it perfectly,' Sally told him. 'I can't understand her...'

'You will—when you're a mother,' Vincent Dunn said with a smile. 'Love plays strange tricks. It's only love for her child and her grandchildren that makes the old lady so difficult. If it wasn't that, I wouldn't have so much patience. Anyhow, we'll see what Dr Chart has to say. I could be wrong, of course.'

'I think it would upset your wife more to be...' Sally began.

He smiled. 'So do I. To dream of a day and then, at the last moment, to have it postponed...' He glanced at his watch. 'I must hurry.'

He opened the door and then looked back. 'Be an angel, Sally, and ring Dr Chart and ask him if he could oblige me by coming to lunch. Don't tell him why. I don't want to prejudice him either way. Just say it's important but we won't keep him long. That man's a demon for work—certainly keeps the hospital staff on their toes...' he added, closing the door.

Sally hesitated as she went to the 'phone. Would Bob remember the last time she asked him to come down to see Mrs Cameron's 'patients' and perhaps think that this was another false trail?

She 'phoned the hospital, telling the impersonal voice that answered that she wished to speak to Dr Chart.

'Who's speaking?' the impersonal voice asked coldly.

'Miss Hampton—but I'm speaking for Mr Dunn,' Sally said with equal coolness.

'The doctor is busy. Can I give him a message?'

Sally hesitated. 'Yes. Would you say that Mr Dunn has something important to ask him but that, knowing how busy the doctor

167

is, he wondered if he would come to lunch today? Mr Dunn also said that he would not detain him for long,' Sally said stiffly.

'I've got that down, Miss Hampton,' the impersonal voice said. 'I'll see that the doctor gets the message.'

'Thank you...' Sally said, ringing off.

Putting down the receiver, she wondered who it was on the 'phone. Another new nurse, perhaps. The nursing staff was always changing for, though the salaries were good, many of the nurses found that life on an island was not the paradise they had expected. However, Mr Dunn had remarked recently that the staff were no longer leaving so rapidly and he wondered why! He had glanced at his wife with a quick smile as he spoke so perhaps he knew that the nurses found Bob 'smooth' and 'fab'.

Bob had just finished his morning round when the freckled, red-headed nurse came running down the corridor after him.

'A 'phone message, sir...' she was saying.

He stopped and waited. He had slept little the night before and felt in no mood for coy smiles and fluttering eye-lashes. Even as he thought this, he felt ashamed of himself. Was he growing so conceited these days that he imagined every nurse was chasing him? Maybe his subconscious mind was giving him a boost to repair the damage done to his ego by Sally. The thought made him smile and to his dismay, he saw the girl's green eyes brighten. It took so little to encourage them.

'It was from a Miss Hampton, sir...' she said and picked a piece of paper from the pocket of her apron.

Sally! Now what would she be 'phoning him about, Bob wondered. He stood patiently as the girl read out:

'Mr Dunn has something important to ask but knowing how busy the doctor is, wondered if he'd come to lunch but will not detain him for long.'

Bob frowned. 'Miss Hampton said that?'

The girl looked at him and smiled. 'She sounded mad because I wouldn't call you to the 'phone.'

'Where was I?'

'On your round, Doctor, and you know you've expressly said there must be no interruptions unless they're important...'

'But this was important,' Bob said irritably. 'Miss Hampton said so ... Thanks, anyhow...' he added and strode down the corridor to his room, glancing at his watch.

Stupid ass of a girl! He'd have to hustle or he'd be late and it must be important for Vincent Dunn to ask him to lunch, for he knew it was often the hospital's busiest part of the day

Twenty minutes later, Bob drew up outside the 'glass house', parking the

169

hospital's car under the great thatched car port. As usual the front door was open and he walked through to the terrace where everyone was sitting.

'I'm sorry I'm late, sir,' Bob said to Vincent Dunn. 'I've only just got your message.'

Vincent Dunn put down his glass and frowned, glancing at Sally. 'But I asked you...'

'It wasn't Sally's fault, sir,' Bob said hastily. 'Some stupid nurse took it on herself not to deliver the message until I'd been round the wards. She ought to have known better,' he added crossly.

'Well, I know you've no time to waste, Chart, so let's go in and lunch, now, and we can talk about the problem as we eat,' Dunn said.

The large dining-room was pleasantly cool after the humid heat outside, the windows opened to any breeze that might blow, the table bright with beautifully prepared food.

The Dunns certainly lived well, Bob was thinking, as he followed the family inside. He noted that Mrs Ester's mouth was like a zipped bag, thin and irritated, that George's face was rather too red for his physical condition, that Louella Dunn was not far from tears and her husband obviously controlling annoyance. Bob wondered what the 'problem' was. He glanced at Sally but she avoided his eyes and looked at her plate demurely.

After a delicious iced soup, they had creamed shrimp curry, and Vincent Dunn glanced at Bob.

'You are aware that my wife's six months ends tomorrow?'

Bob smiled. 'I certainly am.' He looked at Louella Dunn. 'I bet you're counting the hours until tomorrow.'

He saw, to his dismay, that her eyes were filled with tears as she nodded silently.

Mrs Ester spoke abruptly and Bob understood what the 'problem' was!

'I don't think she should just get up, Dr Chart,' Mrs Ester said crossly. 'She's weak from her long time in bed and it would be absolutely foolish to do too much to start with. If she got up one hour a day to begin with . . .'

Bob chose his words carefully. 'But Mrs Ester, your daughter hasn't been ill. Physically ill.'

'Why was she told to rest for six months, then?' the thin sunken cheeks of the old woman were flushed. 'If she wasn't ill . . .'

Again he had to choose his words carefully. 'Your daughter was having attacks of migraine and unpleasant black-outs because she was undergoing severe emotional strain. The complete rest was advised so that her body could relax and give

171

her time to overcome the strain. As you know, she has not been under any drugs, not even sedation recently. There has been no question of any fever or physical ailment. Complete rest was recommended and fortunately, Mrs Dunn had the good sense to follow the advice. Today she is as fit and well as you or I.'

Even as he spoke, Bob caught the quick glance that passed between Sally and Vincent Dunn and, for a moment, Bob forgot what he was talking about and knew only the humiliating burning flame of jealousy. So there was something between Dunn and Sally, he told himself, even if neither of them realized it as yet.

'Then I can get up tomorrow?' Louella's eager voice jerked Bob back to the present.

He managed to smile. 'Certainly.' He looked at Mrs Ester. 'Believe me, Mrs Dunn is adult enough to know when she is tired. We—you, as her mother and I, as her doctor—have no means of knowing if she feels tired, exhausted or in need of rest. Your daughter will know and I feel we can trust her to adjust herself accordingly. Not too many late nights for the first few weeks, perhaps. A rest with a book in the afternoon—but definitely, no more than that. That period of Mrs Dunn's life is behind her.'

Even as he stopped speaking, Bob heard

the quick catching of Louella's breath, saw the pleasure on her face. He hoped he had not annoyed Mrs Ester but he had merely told the truth. There was nothing physically wrong with Louella Dunn—no reason at all why she should be tied to a wheel-chair or her bed. If only Mrs Ester could realize how much more of a danger to her daughter's health she was than anything else could be, he thought that things might improve.

This ridiculous possessive protective mother-love was a mistake. Birds tossed their babies out of the nest as soon as they could look after themselves. Parents should do the same. Bring their children up to be independent and able to care for themselves, go on loving them but give them a gentle push to stand on their own. Louella was a classic example of the over-protected child, haunted by a feeling of guilt because of all her mother had done for her—without realizing that her mother's loving possessiveness was actually a form of selfishness, a refusal to break the natal cord that bound them.

Bob looked across the table at Vincent Dunn. 'You wanted to ask me about something, sir?'

Vincent did not smile. 'You've told us what we want to know, Doctor, thank you. I just wanted to make sure my wife could get up tomorrow and lead a normal life.'

Bob looked at him thoughtfully. 'Your wife is a fit woman and her life, as from now on, can be completely normal.' He glanced at his watch. 'If you'll excuse me...'

'Of course ... of course,' Vincent Dunn said and escorted Bob to the door. Bob was surprised when Vincent walked with him to the car, even more surprised when Vincent said quietly:

'Will my wife ever be a normal woman so long as her mother lives with us?'

Bob's hands were on the steering wheel, the car's engine purring gently, as he looked up at the worried face of the man waiting for his answer. In the background, was the distant roar of the ocean pounding relentlessly against the reef, the usual faint drift of music on the air, the sweet sickly smell of flowers.

'It's not easy to define the word "normal", sir,' Bob said.

'But her mother does constitute...'

'A very real danger to your wife's happiness and consequently, to her health,' Bob finished the sentence. He looked down at his hands for a moment and glanced up. 'It's a difficult situation, sir. Your wife has a guilt complex where her mother is concerned—to forcibly cut the cord that binds them would not help matters. The time will come when your wife will see...' Bob hesitated. 'I don't know how to put

174

this,' he said unhappily. 'What I'm getting at is...'

'That one day she'll have to choose between us?' Vincent Dunn said bluntly.

Bob switched off the engine and heard the sound of the surf more clearly.

'She loves you very much...'

'But she loves her mother more...' Vincent parried.

Startled, Bob looked up. 'Oh no, sir...' he said quickly. 'Definitely not but...'

'She finds it easier to hurt me than to hurt her mother?'

'Because her mother shows she is hurt whereas you hide your pain,' Bob said and lifted his hand before Vincent could speak. 'Please let me finish. This is a problem that constantly arises and is not easy to solve. If you spoke bluntly and said her mother must go, your wife would agree but she would never be able to forgive...'

'Me?'

'No, herself. She's torn in two. Between her loyalty and what she believes she owes her mother and her love for you and her longing and need to be alone with you. It is just tearing her apart. The fact that she really wants her mother to leave you alone together, merely makes the matter more involved and her decision harder to take.'

'You sound sorry for her,' Vincent said drily.

Bob glanced at him. 'I am...' He gave a wry smile. 'I'm also damned sorry for you, sir.'

Vincent smiled. 'Any solution?'

Bob shrugged helplessly. 'I think one day something will blow up—I don't know how or when. But your wife will then have to make her choice...'

'And how does the betting go on that?' Vincent asked with a strange smile.

Bob switched on the engine and grinned. 'I'm betting on you, sir.'

Vincent Dunn stood back and lifted his hand. 'Thanks, Bob. Then you advise patience?'

Bob nodded. 'Afraid so, sir. Thanks...' he added as he drove away.

Sally could hear the roar of the car's engine as she finished lunch silently. She wondered what Mr Dunn and Bob could have found to talk about for so long.

Vaguely she heard Louella Dunn and her mother talking. Mrs Ester seemed less irritable, but said that she did hope her daughter had the common sense with which the doctor credited her, and Louella was laughing and saying that of course she had.

Sally could feel her whole body relaxing slowly. It was odd what an effect being in the same room with Bob had on her. She had been so tensed; unable to look at him, yet longing to do so. Listening to his voice—hoping he would speak to her, yet afraid he might read the truth in her eyes.

'I can't wait until tomorrow...' Louella was saying excitedly. 'Vincent's bought me a new dress for the occasion and we're having champagne to celebrate.'

'The money that man wastes...' Mrs Ester said dourly.

Louella's laugh rang out. 'But he wastes it in such a nice way Mother, you must admit that...'

Sally, pushing Mrs Dunn's wheel-chair, sympathized with her whole-heartedly. How on earth would she like it, she wondered, if she was condemned for six months to bed and a wheel-chair! Surely Mrs Ester could understand Louella's desire to walk about, to dance, to do all the things she had been forbidden to do for six months?

Back on the terrace, the sun no longer so fierce as a sea breeze had sprung up, Sally thought how well Bob had handled the situation. No hesitation at all. His voice firm and authoritative, his manner professional yet compassionate. She thought that if she was ill, the mere fact of having Bob as her doctor would make her feel better at once. Or to work with him ... No wonder, the nurses at the hospital drooled about him, as Beryl had once said, and had then added with an odd smile at Sally that she did not blame them.

The next morning dawned fair and bright. Sally stood by the window gazing at the wonderful panorama of blue water, white sand, the sails of some early yachtsmen—was Bob one of them, she wondered—at the colour of the flowers, the sound of the surf. She dressed swiftly and hurried to Louella Dunn's room.

Louella was already up and dressed, her eyes bright with excitement. She wore her new dress. A very light batiste that was the personification of coolness and a deep warm amber colour. Her hair was elaborately done. her face perfectly made-up and she was walking about the room. As she saw Sally, she came to meet her, kissed her warmly.

'I'm out of prison at last...' she said happily.

All through the day, Sally watched the careful way Louella Dunn behaved. Resting on her couch on the terrace after lunch with a book but talking to her mother most of the time.

When Johnny came home from school with Beryl, both came out to the terrace and their mother walked across the tiles to kiss them.

'You're back again, Mummy,' Johnny said, excitedly. 'Will you come for a walk?'

'Of course, darling,' his mother said and

kissed him again. 'Granny was just telling me something. As soon as she's finished, we'll go...' she promised.

Sally saw the quickly-hidden, sceptical smile Beryl gave before she turned to go indoors but Johnny sat patiently on the wall of the terrace.

'As I was saying, Louella...' Mrs Ester said, her voice faintly exasperated. 'When your father...'

Sally slipped away to her room. She must write to her grandfather. He wrote regularly and she knew he enjoyed her letters. As his eyesight was deteriorating, she always used a very thick black pencil, more of a crayon than a pencil, and would print the words. This took longer, so she usually wrote her letters in several instalments, as she knew he often read them aloud to his friends.

There was always plenty to tell him. Of Johnny's absorption in tikis and *tupapaus*—of the people of the island and their songs and dances—of the outrigger canoes that went out with fishermen—of the circular nets that many used from shore—the yachts that moored in the harbour, the visitors that came.

It was an hour and a half later that Sally went back to the terrace, for she usually poured out the tea and handed round the delicate bread and butter rolls that Mrs Ester liked and the crisp gingerbread biscuits

Johnny loved.

Johnny was still sitting on the terrace wall, his face patient, his hands clasped round his knees, his eyes fixed on his mother. She was leaning back in her couch-chair, eyes half-closed and Mrs Ester was still talking.

Even as Sally joined them, the tea trolleys were wheeled out. Johnny came to her side and took three gingerbread biscuits, looked at his mother, gave a tiny shrug of his thin shoulders and walked off. Sally watched him go and felt sorry for him, not sure if she should remind his mother of her forgotten promise, not wanting to interrupt the conversation.

Mrs Ester was talking about a great uncle of hers and his three wives. 'Not one of them gave him a child...' she was saying.

Sally handed round the tea and then slipped back to her room to finish the letter.

It was a gay dinner-party, simply the family and Sally. Champagne—liqueurs with black coffee—and then the new records Vincent Dunn had bought on his latest trip to Papeete.

Sally, sitting quietly, saw Louella Dunn suddenly frown and went quickly to her side.

'Do you want something?' Sally asked softly.

Louella Dunn's face was troubled. 'Sally,' she said quietly, because Mrs Ester disapproved of people talking when music

180

was being played, 'I've just remembered I promised to go for a walk with Johnny and I forgot. Could you slip up to his room and tell him I'm sorry and I won't forget tomorrow?' Her eyes looked appealingly at Sally. 'It's so difficult to stop Mother when she gets going about the family and...'

'I know. I'll go and tell him,' Sally said. She hesitated. Then smiled. 'Johnny'll understand.'

'Yes, bless him,' Louella said.

Sally wondered if Johnny would still be awake as she went up the stairs. She opened Johnny's door gently. It was in darkness but the light from the landing shone directly on to the bed.

The bed was empty.

CHAPTER TEN

Bob straightened his aching back and glanced round at the red-headed nurse, whose name was, he had learned, Sara Gough, and frowned as she hurried towards him.

'Now what is it?' he growled and then wished he hadn't for she was tired as he was. Both had been working in the theatre in a vain attempt to save the life of a child who had been hurt by a runaway tractor. Now he was working on the driver.

'It's no good—I'll have to operate...' Bob said wearily, brushing his hand across his face. 'Get a message to Matron, nurse, please.'

'Excuse me, sir...' she persisted. 'An important 'phone call just came for you.'

'Oh no...' he groaned. 'It can't be that important.'

'It's from the same girl,' Nurse Gough said, her voice slightly amused. 'Last time you were mad at me for not telling you.'

Bob's stiff face grimaced. 'And this time I'm mad at you for telling me ... I know. You just can't win, eh, nurse?' He glanced at his watch. Nearly ten o'clock. What on earth could Sally want at this hour, he wondered.

He was aware that the nurse was watching his face interestedly. He sighed.

'I'd better take it, I suppose. Get things started for me, please, nurse. We'd better not waste much time.'

He padded along to the 'phone.

'Sally? Bob here...' he said.

At first he couldn't make out a word of what she was trying to say. The words just tumbled out of her lips, all mixed up.

'Hey, steady on,' he said sharply. 'Pull yourself together, Sally. What's happened?'

He heard her gasp and then her voice sobered. 'I'm sorry, Bob, just got a bit upset. You see, when she forgot, I was half-afraid something would happen and I wondered if I ought to remind her and I didn't and now, I'm wondering...'

'Whoa back...' he said angrily. 'Look, Sally, I've a man dying on my hands, waiting for me to operate. Calm down or I'll ring off. What's happened?'

'Johnny's vanished...' she told him bluntly.

'Vanished? Nonsense. Probably in the bathroom...' he said. What a fuss about nothing, he thought. A ten-year-old boy didn't just vanish!

'I've looked—everywhere. I even went outside in case he'd gone fishing or something but he hasn't taken his fishing things and besides, he's never done such a thing before...' Sally's voice was unsteady.

'There always has to be a first time,' Bob said shortly. 'Get on with the story. How did you discover he was missing? Try and keep it short and let me have the picture,' he said crossly.

He could hear her draw a long deep breath and so he added, his voice more gentle, 'Steady, old girl. Young boys often disappear and turn up a few hours later. He's growing up, you know, and it could be a sign of independence.'

'But ... all right, Bob. This afternoon when Johnny came home from school, he asked his mother to go for a walk. She said she would and forgot all about it. An hour and a half, or maybe two hours later, he stopped waiting. I saw him look at her, shrug his shoulders and go off. Just ... just now, Mrs Dunn remembered her promise and was rather upset. She asked me to go and explain to him. I went and ... and he wasn't there.'

'And you're afraid he's run off in a tantrum?' Bob asked, his voice dry.

'I ... I don't know what I'm afraid of,' Sally said. 'I only know that I don't want to be the person to tell his mother that he's not in bed. I can just imagine Mrs Ester...'

'Quite. She'd probably put pressure on, for I know she dislikes Masters. She'd say it was his influence. Johnny had never been like that, before,' Bob said. 'I get the point, Sally, that's what you were thinking, eh?'

'Bob, I don't know what I'm thinking,' Sally said. 'I only know I'm worried and don't know what to do next...'

'Sally, I can't get down in less than an hour, maybe two. I've got a pretty big job on hand right now,' Bob said thoughtfully. 'I suggest you contact Masters. He knows Johnny well, probably has a better idea of what a small boy would do. Frankly, I don't think Johnny would run away to frighten his mother simply because she forgot to keep a promise. She's forgotten too many in the past for it to upset him...'

'Bob,' Sally gasped. He heard the shock in

her voice. 'How can you—?'

'Isn't it true?' he asked. 'Look, Sally, we've been over this before. Louella loves her husband. She only had the children to please him. She admitted it. She is not the maternal type. I don't think Johnny's run away...' He spoke more slowly as he tried to think aloud.

'Sally—I've got a hunch. It may be no good but it might be a lead. Ask Masters about it. Remember the time we went round the island and Johnny came along, talking about ghosts and tikis and what-nots? I have a hunch it's something to do with that. Anyhow, talk it over with Masters and...' He dropped his crisp voice and spoke more gently. 'Don't worry, Sally. Little boys are tough. We'll find him. Just think up something to keep Louella happy and get in touch with Masters and I'll be down the instant I can. Okay?'

'Okay...' she said and he wondered at the weariness in her voice and then there was a click as she rang off.

He hesitated, tempted to ring her back. But what could he do, he asked himself. The man with a brain injury needed him first. As he left the office, the little red-headed nurse came bustling towards him.

'Everything's under control, sir...' she said.

He managed a grin. 'Good work, nurse,' he said.

185

*   *   *

Sally put down the receiver slowly. She felt just as if Bob had slapped her face. The next moment, she told herself that she was being unfair, unreasonable. Bob was a doctor—his work must come first. A man's life might be in the balance...

But so might Johnny's, she thought miserably. Her hands were damp with fear, her mouth dry. What was she to tell them? She hesitated, imagining the scene that awaited her if she told the truth?

Quietly she went into the lounge; the tall vases of flowers were bright against the silver-white walls, the deep gold of the curtains warm in the lights that shone from the silver sconces on the walls. A mixture of contemporary furniture and gracious antiques had, somehow, made it all into a very lovely room.

Mr Dunn and George Ester were talking. Mrs Ester was playing patience, studying the cards on the table before her. Louella Dunn was sitting very upright, her smile a little too bright, Sally thought.

Quietly Sally went to Louella Dunn's side. 'I didn't wake him...' she said softly. It was a form of truth, even though not the whole truth.

Louella's eyes brightened. 'Never mind, Sally, I'll tell him myself tomorrow. Thanks

186

for going up.'

'I've got a frightful headache,' Sally said and this time it was a real lie. 'If you don't mind, I think I'll have an early night.'

'Of course. Want some aspirin? You've got some? See you in the morning,' Louella Dunn said with a smile. 'Good night.'

'Thanks. Goodnight...' Sally said and slipped quietly out of the room.

In the hall, she went straight to the drawer where the keys of the cars were kept. Equally quietly, she slipped out of the house and went to the car she was allowed to use.

The engine seemed to roar terribly as she started it and for a moment, she was scared lest Mr Dunn hear it and come out to see who it was. Her hands were shaking as she drove away and she did not relax until the car was climbing the side of the strange narrow mountain and she knew that no one had seen her leave.

How casually Bob had 'tossed the baby' to Paddy, she thought. Ask Masters, he had said. He understands little boys. Why did Bob always have to use that condescending voice when he spoke of Paddy? And suppose Paddy was out? He was not on the 'phone so she had no choice but to try to find him. Beryl was out somewhere, too, but it was unlikely that Beryl would be with Paddy, for the two rarely got on together.

The sight of the neat, compact thatched

roof cottage was a welcome one to Sally. Carefully she drove off the main road below the school and drove between rows of huge tropical plants towards the cottage. There was a light burning and as she stopped the car, Paddy opened the door and came out.

'Visitors? What fun!' he began and stopped as he saw her face in the light from the cottage. 'What's wrong, Sally?' he asked.

He helped her out of the car and into the cottage. Her legs seemed to be shaking and she was glad of his helping arm round her. Inside there was one big room, a skylight in the roof, easels at one end, a couch at the other. Several huge armchairs and a table.

Paddy made her sit down and in a moment, handed her a glass.

'Drink that and you'll feel better,' he said curtly.

Sally obeyed. The liquid was fiery and made her choke and cough but it warmed her and some of the shakiness left her. Soon she could tell him what had happened. Bob's angry words had made her realize the necessity for wasting no time on hysterics. His anger had hurt her immeasurably. Somehow she had turned to him for help without thinking of anyone else, so sure had she been that he would understand and help her. Instead, he had been curt and annoyed with her and had passed her on to Paddy. Yet was that really fair of her, she asked herself. Bob was a doctor and his patient must come first. Yet she still felt hurt about it.

Paddy listened silently, sitting on the edge of a chair, hands loosely clasped between his knees, his eyes on her.

'And they don't know Johnny isn't in bed?' he asked.

'No, I just said I hadn't woken him,' Sally explained. 'I was afraid if I told the truth that Mrs Ester would make a scene, Mrs Dunn get all upset and ... Honestly, Paddy, I didn't know what to do.'

'So you came to me?' Paddy asked, his eyes narrowed.

'No, I rang Bob first but he couldn't help. He's operating and ... and he told me to come to you,' Sally admitted.

Paddy looked thoughtful. 'He did, now? Why?'

'He said you'd understand little boys better than he does. He said my idea was nonsense...'

'Your idea?' Paddy stood up, refilled the glasses and sat down again. 'Relax, Sally,' he said. 'Ten minutes isn't going to matter. What was your idea?'

Sally told him about Johnny and his mother's promise.

'He waited so patiently, without worrying anyone, and then shrugged his shoulders and walked off. I'm afraid...'

'That he's run away from home to frighten his mother?' Paddy asked. He shook his head. 'Not on your life, Sally. Johnny isn't that type. 'Sides, he's too used to broken promises.' He paused. 'Is that what Bob Chart said?' he asked, noticing the way Sally had blushed.

She nodded unhappily. 'Yes. He said Louella doesn't love the children and that they're used to it.'

'I agree.' Paddy made a great show of lighting a pipe and leaning back in his chair. Sally wanted to jump up, tell him to hurry, to arrange a search party, but she knew he was only trying to make her relax so that he could know the whole story thoroughly.

'Know something, Sally? We often get the boys to write explanations of certain words. One day the word "promise" was chosen. Know what Johnny wrote? He wrote: "A promise is what Mummy makes and forgets to keep and a promise is what Daddy never forgets." That explain everything?'

'Yes but ... She did mean to keep it, it was just her mother...' Sally said quickly.

Paddy lifted a finger. 'Ah, there we have it. The crucial point. Her mother. The children understand and accept Louella's behaviour, as her husband does, but her mother couldn't understand, ever, so Louella falls over backwards to avoid hurting her. Had Bob any bright ideas as to why the boy might

190

have run off?'

Sally sipped her drink and shivered. 'He said to ask you about tikis or some such word. When Johnny came with us, he...' She stopped speaking, put down her glass and leaned forward, her voice changing. 'Paddy, I think I know what Bob meant. Johnny told us that the local boys were terrified of *tupa-*...'

'*Tupapaus?*' Paddy asked.

'Yes, and Johnny said that one day he'd show them he wasn't a coward, like them. I can't remember his words but it was something...'

She stopped speaking for Paddy was on his feet.

'I think I know what Chart was getting at and he could be right. Johnny comes in for quite a lot of ribbing at school. Mrs Ester would probably snatch her darling baby from my arms if she knew but even small boys have to grow up and learn to defend themselves.'

'You mean they bully him?' Sally said, shocked.

Paddy grinned. 'That's too strong a word. They tease him. They tease most of the white boys for if they're obedient, they wear sneakers on the coral. Otherwise you can get some very ugly cuts. Local boys never wear shoes until they're grown up and then only on a Sunday. Lots of small things. Local boys are stronger, of course. From youth, they're used to lifting heavy weights. Maybe Johnny planned to show them he wasn't as superstitious as they are...'

He was on his way to the door, Sally close behind. 'He'll be all right?' she asked.

'Of course,' Paddy said cheerfully. 'We'll find him. I know one *mareu* that all the local lads are terrified of—they say if you spend a night there, you'll wake up in the morning with a head like a melon. I bet he'll be glad to see us, though he won't admit it. It can be pretty eerie in these jungle places.'

'And how!' Sally felt tempted to say, half an hour later, as she followed Paddy along a narrow path, through glades of bushes and trees, so closely interlaced with creepers that sometimes they had to bend down and almost creep to move along the path. It was a hot night, a big red moon flaming in the dark sky. There were odd noises—a sudden crack, the heavy thud of a coconut falling to the ground—the distant screech of an animal.

Paddy had a powerful torch that blazed a light through the darkness ahead but he walked so fast that Sally was breathless as she tried to keep up with him. They seemed to walk for hours and she had soon rubbed a blister on her heel. If she'd only known they were going to walk miles, she thought miserably, she would have changed to low heels.

Paddy stopped abruptly and she bumped into him. His arm went round her and his light went out. He spoke in her ear.

'Don't move. When your eyes are used to the darkness, you'll see him. Just to the left by that huge rock, Sally...'

His arm was warm and comforting round her and she felt some of the fear leave her tired body. She looked in the direction Paddy had told her and gradually as her eyes grew accustomed to the blackness under the trees, she made out the form of a rock vaguely, then a great stone, fashioned roughly she saw, into the shape of a squatting man and just beyond it, wrapped in a blanket, his head hidden from view, a small figure.

'I think we should leave the plucky little devil there,' Paddy said in Sally's ears. 'He must be scared stiff, poor little lad. It seems mean to spoil it for him.'

'But suppose they find he's not in his bedroom?' Sally whispered back. 'Won't he get the same kudos from his friends at school if you say you had to *make* him go home?'

Paddy's arm tightened round her. 'You're a sweet thing, Sally.' His mouth brushed her ear gently. 'I guess you're right. The kid's proved his toughness. Now we'll walk back a way and I'll call his name. He must never know that we saw him with the blanket over his head.'

193

Obediently she stumbled back down the path and Paddy began shouting, faintly at first, and then louder, switching on his light, flashing it round everywhere.

At last it shone on Johnny's flushed startled face.

'So there you are, my pesky lad...' Paddy said, striding into the clearing. 'And what, may I ask, are you up to, here?'

'Sally...' Johnny said, startled. 'Oh dear, I meant to be home before breakfast, Sally. I only have to stay here till the dawn.'

'I don't think they know you're not in bed,' Sally said and saw the relief on his face.

'Mummy would be awful upset,' he told her.

Sally nodded. 'She sent me up to tell you she was sorry she forgot about the walk ... that's how I found you were missing.'

'I bet you're here to show your face isn't big as a water melon,' Paddy said.

Johnny went bright red. 'They call me chicken 'cos I wear sneakers on the rocks...'

'They're fools because they don't,' Paddy said. 'Come along, young man, time you were tucked up in bed.'

'But I must stay here...' Johnny said desperately.

'I won't let you,' Paddy said firmly. 'Tomorrow, I shall tell class what a bad boy you are, planning to sleep the night in a *mareu* next door to a tiki and with all the *tupapaus* around to play tricks on you. I'll say I marched you home against your will and they'll never call you chicken again.'

In the brightness of the flashlight, Sally saw the way Johnny's eyes were shining.

'Then I'll be brave?'

'You won't *be*...' Paddy said. 'You *are*. Remember that, Johnny.'

In an incredibly short time, Sally and Johnny were leaving Paddy at his cottage door, getting into Sally's car, and on their way home.

'I hope Mummy doesn't know,' Johnny said, curled up by her side, yawning.

'She'd be proud of you if she did,' Sally said. 'But next time. Johnny, you do anything like this, let me know first.'

'Dad might be proud but Mummy wouldn't understand,' Johnny went on. 'She'd only be worried in case Granny found out, for Granny'd be awful mad about it.'

'Yes, well, maybe Granny needn't ever know,' Sally said slowly. Mrs Ester would, Sally was thinking, seize the opportunity to blame Paddy for teaching the children about tikis, *pareus* and *tupapaus*! She might even pressure Mrs Dunn enough to make her take Johnny away from the school.

For the last part of the way home, Sally free-wheeled, hoping no one would hear the car. The front door was, as always unlocked and they crept into the house, Johnny's hand

195

warm and sticky in hers, as they went to the kitchen part and up the back staircase.

The corridor to Johnny's bedroom was deserted and Sally tucked him up in bed, kissed him goodnight, and left the room. She had taken only a few steps when a door on the other side of the corridor opened. Sally stiffened and there was a silence that seemed to last forever. At last, she managed to turn round and found herself gazing at Vincent Dunn.

He was still dressed, a cigarette in his hand.

'What on earth have you been up to?' he asked, his voice low.

'I ... I've just been out...' Sally stammered, her voice as quiet as his.

'Where—with whom?' Mr Dunn asked, his voice unusually stern. 'Have you any idea what you look like, Sally?'

Her cheeks hot, Sally glanced down at her pink frock. It was torn by the creepers she had fought; crumpled and dirty. She lifted a hand to her hair and found it tangled and knew that it—and she—must look a mess.

'I went for ... for a drive and...' Sally began.

Both heard a door quietly opening; at the same moment, both turned just as a small hot hand slid into Sally's.

'It's not her fault, Daddy,' Johnny said in a hoarse, nervous whisper. 'She was out
196

rescuing me.'

'Rescuing you? From what?' his father asked, his voice like steel.

'It's an ... an awful long story,' Johnny whispered.

'I still think I'd better hear it,' his father said, leading the way back to Johnny's room, closing the door when they were all inside, looking down at his son. 'Well, let's hear it.'

Johnny's hand clung to Sally's but his voice was steady as he told his father of the boys who called him chicken, of his scorn for them because they feared the *tupapaus* and how he planned to prove that he wasn't scared.

'It was awful dark and kind of scary, Dad, but I knew I had to show them I wasn't a coward,' Johnny finished.

'I see,' his father said. 'I quite see how you felt, Johnny, and I'm not mad at you but—did you think of how your mother would have worried if she'd known you were out all night?'

'How would she know, Daddy?' Johnny asked. 'No one comes to my room once I'm in bed.'

Vincent Dunn glanced for a second at Sally. Sally wondered if he had also heard the faintly wistful note in Johnny's voice. Had she unwittingly treated the small boy as being older than he was, Sally asked herself. Ought she to have automatically gone in every night, to tell him a story and tuck him up? It was his mother's job, of course, but then she had been an invalid for six months.

'How did you know he'd gone, Sally?' Vincent Dunn asked.

Once again, Sally reluctantly told of the forgotten promise by Johnny's mother, of her request to Sally to go and ask Johnny to forgive her.

'I found he wasn't in his room or—anywhere,' she finished.

'What did you do?'

Sally swallowed nervously. Maybe she had done the wrong thing, she thought. 'I rang Bob—I mean Dr Chart.'

'Why?'

Sally's face was suddenly hot. 'I don't know,' she confessed. 'I just ... just did.'

'And Dr Chart?'

'Was about to operate and said he couldn't leave the hospital,' Sally said. 'He suggested I got in touch with Paddy ... Mr Masters. Bob ... Bob thought he might know more about little boys...' She squeezed Johnny's hand in apology. 'Bob also suggested it might be to do with tikis and *tupapaus*. It was his idea and when I told Paddy, he knew at once where to go and we did and...'

'You found Johnny.' Vincent Dunn said. He ruffled Johnny's hair gently. 'Maybe I should be cross, Johnny, but I'm proud of you, son. Next time, though, let me know when you're going to do anything like this. I can keep a secret.'

'I know you can, Daddy. And you're not cross with Sally?' Johnny asked.

'Cross...?' Vincent Dunn's voice was odd. 'How could I be? I'm grateful.' He tucked the boy in bed and kissed him, then turned to Sally.

'If his mother had known or Madre had found out...' he said quietly. 'All hell would have been let loose.'

'I know. That's what scared me. I didn't want it to happen on Mrs Dunn's first day up...' Sally agreed.

''Night, Johnny,' Vincent Dunn said, switching off the light, opening the door. He walked down the corridor to Sally's room and then turned to look down at her.

'Sally,' he said gently. 'I can only say thank you—thank you very much indeed.'

His hands were on her shoulders, holding her gently but firmly, and he bent and kissed her on the mouth.

'Thank you very much indeed,' he repeated and then turned and left her.

Sally opened her door and walked into her dark bedroom, closing the door behind her, putting out her hand to switch on the light.

The touch of Mr Dunn's mouth was still warm on hers—but most of all she remembered the look in his eyes. He had been so grateful that he had not known what to do or say—because, like her, he had known what a fuss Mrs Ester would have made about the innocent little escapade if she had had the chance.

Sally began to undress quickly. What a brave boy Johnny was, she thought, remembering the huddled figure under the blanket, the courage in his voice as he had confessed the truth to his father. Never again, at school, Paddy had said, would Johnny be called 'chicken'.

CHAPTER ELEVEN

Bob stood very still, at the top of the curving staircase as he watched Sally enter her room and close her door, and saw Vincent Dunn walk to his room and go inside.

Bob was shocked to find he was shaking, his hands clenched into angry fists. He had seen it with his own eyes ... Dunn had kissed Sally, he kept telling himself.

And what was even worse, he thought, Sally had made no attempt to stop him.

Suddenly life seemed to flow back into Bob's veins and he turned aside to go down the stairs—and froze as he heard yet another door quietly close.

He swung round, looking down the

200

corridor but all was still—the doors looking like blank uninterested eyes. It must have been his imagination, he told himself.

He was so tired he could hardly keep his eyes open, so exhausted was he that it had been a real effort to drive down to find out if Johnny was all right. Not wanting to disturb anyone, he had walked quietly up the stairs to look in the boy's room and had reached the top of the staircase just in time to see...

Bob swallowed, forcing himself to walk quietly down the stairs, go out to his car and drive back to the hospital. Never in his life, could he remember feeling so angry. Just wait until he saw Sally...

Bob realized suddenly that he was driving recklessly, going too fast round the steep bends. On a sudden impulse, he turned off the main road and made his way to the school and Masters' cottage. There was a light burning and Paddy Masters came outside when he heard the car. His light hair was ruffled, he was yawning; he had pulled an old bathrobe on over his green pyjamas.

'Everything's okay, Doc...' he called out. 'Thanks to you, we found Johnny.'

Bob found it difficult to speak normally. His whole body felt taut as a wrenched wire. 'Where was he?' he asked.

Paddy told him. 'Gallant little idiot,' Paddy finished. 'But thanks for the clue. I doubt if I'd have thought he had the guts.'

'Johnny's all right,' Bob said slowly.

Paddy gave him a quick glance. 'You mad about something?'

Bob tried to smile but his face was stiff with weariness. 'No, just bushed. Had a hard day and then this. Sally ... she sounded very upset...'

'I think she'd calmed down by the time she got here,' Paddy said. 'We came back with the kid and she drove him home.'

'Was she going to tell his father?'

Paddy ran his hand through his hair. 'I guess she'll get Johnny to tell him tomorrow. She won't risk waking up the old dragon tonight—or the whole point in Operation Rescue...' he added with a grin, 'would be done away with.'

Bob started the engine again. 'Quite. Thanks, anyhow, Paddy.'

Paddy grinned. ''Bye, Bob.'

Bob realized with a shock that it was the first time they had used Christian names. It was odd, he realized, as he drove back to the hospital more slowly but for the first time, he'd liked Paddy Masters.

He smiled wryly as he swung round a sharp U-bend. What would Paddy say, he wondered, if he knew the truth? That their innocent little Sally was in love with Vincent Dunn and that they had already reached the stage when Dunn could kiss her without protest...

The anger flared again and he tried to quieten it. He told himself that jealousy was for the immature. He had no right to be jealous. Sally was not his girl. She had never pretended to be interested in him. He had never told her he loved her, so what excuse could he find for his anger?

He saw the hospital ahead and longed for his bed. At least he'd feel better about it in the morning. Maybe there was a reason for that kiss...

He slammed on the brakes and skidded to a careless halt under the carport. What excuse could there be, he asked himself.

He walked into the hospital and was halfway to his room when Matron opened her door and stopped him. Her face was lined and grey with tiredness, her eyes compassionate.

'I'm sorry, Doctor, but...'

He yawned. 'Don't tell me. Another baby impatient to come into the world?'

Matron smiled. 'Afraid so...'

'Oh well, can't blame the kid, can we?' Bob said. 'I'll just wash up, be with you in a jiffy...'

It was a long hard labour, the mother a young girl of sixteen, scared and needing constant reassurance from the doctor; a husband, not very much older; both just recently out from England and not used to the humidity and heat, but at last Bob could

203

tumble into bed and was instantly asleep.

It hardly seemed a second before someone was shaking his shoulder. Bob blinked, saw everything in a blur and gradually his eyes focused properly and he recognized Matron's face.

'It's about Mrs Dunn, Doctor. I can't get any sense out of her mother but she's almost in hysterics,' she said.

Bob sat up, closing his eyes against the glare from the window. 'What on earth's the time?' He was shocked when he saw the hands of the clock. 'Twelve? Hi, Matron, you should have called me sooner...'

Matron smiled. 'Everything's under control here so I let you sleep. You needed it.'

Bob yawned, rubbed his eyes and stretched. 'I most certainly did. I wonder what's wrong with Mrs Dunn? It was her mother who called?'

'Yes. She said Mr Dunn had gone to Papeete on business—that Mrs Dunn can't swallow properly and finds it hard to breathe.'

'Ring back and say I'll be there right away...' Bob said.

He was accustomed to showering and dressing in a minimum of time and drove fast, reaching the 'glass house' in an incredibly short space of time.

Mrs Ester was coming down the stairs as

he walked in. Her face was white with fear.

'She can't swallow even a spoonful of water, doctor ... I don't know what's happened. I knew she shouldn't get up yesterday. It was all too much for her—the excitement and all.' Mrs Ester's usually authoritative voice was uncertain and afraid. 'Is it a sort of paralysis?'

'I can't tell until I see her,' Bob said. He paused as he was passing her. 'Has anything happened to upset Mrs Dunn?' he asked sharply.

He surprised a quick flash on the old lady's face.

'Nothing at all,' Mrs Ester said sharply but he knew, somehow, that she was lying. 'What could have happened?'

He stared at her thoughtfully, his eyes narrowing. Once again, in his thoughts, he was climbing these same stairs but it was midnight, and at the top he had stopped dead for in front of him he had seen Dunn and Sally—and Dunn was kissing her. He had heard their two doors close and then, as he turned away, had heard another door close. Or had, he corrected himself, thought he had.

Could the third door have been Mrs Ester's? Yet surely even she would not...

He began to run up the stairs, stopped halfway and looked back. 'Is Sally with her?' he asked.

Again he surprised a look on Mrs Ester's face which she was quick to hide. 'No, she isn't,' Mrs Ester said, snapping her mouth together as if trying to gain control of herself. Then added. 'She went into Papeete with Mr Dunn this morning...'

'That's unusual, isn't it?' Bob said without thinking and was annoyed with himself as he saw Mrs Ester's eyes light up as if she had noticed something. It was generally recognized that Rosalie went with Mr Dunn to Papeete for she was his P.A. ... 'A sudden decision, I suppose,' Bob added and thought how lame it sounded and that his words had not helped, might, indeed, have made things worse.

Mrs Ester's mouth was a thin line.

'It was. Very sudden, indeed,' she said, with emphasis on the word 'very'. 'As you know, Rosalie usually goes but it seems that this time, Mr Dunn thought Sally might enjoy a change of ... I believe he called it, locale—whatever he means by that,' she said sourly.

She paused and added, almost reluctantly, he thought:

'He did ask Louella but I advised her against it. I mean, yesterday was tiring enough. Besides...' She stopped and her face coloured.

Bob wondered what she had been going to say and why she looked so relieved because she had stopped herself in time.

Now she frowned. 'Really, Dr Chart,' she said acidly, 'wouldn't it be wiser if you saw your patient instead of wasting time chatting to me?'

He wondered. Maybe he was learning more from this casual chat than Mrs Ester realized, Bob thought. He turned away and agreed:

'You're right, Mrs Ester. You don't seem able to help me with my prognosis.'

As he went upstairs, he thought rapidly of what he knew of Mrs Dunn's medical history. He had already formed a snap judgment as to what was the matter, but a physical examination and a more thorough investigation was needed before he could be certain.

He opened the door to Mrs Dunn's room and paused in the doorway. She lay in bed, propped upright by pillows, her eyes shut, her face drained of all colour, her mouth open as she breathed noisily through her nose.

'Mrs Dunn...' he said gently and went to sit by her side, his hand closing over her wrist. 'Mrs Dunn.' He raised his voice slightly and saw by the flicker of her eyelids that she could hear him. 'Not to worry, Mrs Dunn,' he went on, his voice more confident. 'There's nothing wrong with you that we can't put right...'

*   *   *

Sally had not seen Mr Dunn during the journey back from Papeete. Now she leaned on the rail of the schooner and watched the angular mountain of Mahane Island become more clear on the horizon. Drifts of cloud circled it, making it look strangely unreal. Sally had enjoyed her day in Papeete. Mr Dunn had left her immediately they arrived and she had not seen him again until they were back on the schooner. He had looked tired, had said it had been a hard busy day and he hoped she had enjoyed hers. She had, she had told him, and it was the truth. She had hired a carriage and been driven quite a long way, had looked at the shops, lunched in a very attractive café overlooking the ocean. But she was equally happy to be going back to the island. Mr Dunn had vanished, with a murmured apology, to work out some figures in the cabin and it was only now, as the schooner approached the opening in the reef and they could see the wharf and the cars parked there and the people moving around, that Mr Dunn reappeared.

It was Sally who saw Rosalie first.

'Did you expect her to meet us?' Sally asked, after she had pointed out Rosalie.

He was frowning. 'Certainly not. She hasn't been well, lately, and I gave her the day off. I wonder what can be wrong?'

208

They were soon to find out. Even as the schooner berthed and the first gangway went down, Rosalie came hurrying along it, going straight to them her face worried, her eyes behind her thick-rimmed glasses anxious.

'I'm afraid it's your wife, Mr Dunn. They've taken her to the hospital,' she said breathlessly. 'Dr Chart asked me to notify you immediately and take you there.'

Sally saw the shocked fear on Vincent Dunn's face.

'She had an accident?' he asked.

Rosalie shook her head, her dark fringe and straight hair giving her a mournful look. 'They don't know what happened, but she can't swallow and is having difficulty in breathing.'

'You've got the car waiting—?' he asked, turning to Sally. 'See that my things come ashore. I left them in the cabin,' he said curtly. 'Come on, Rosalie. You'd better drive me.'

They were both down the gangway quickly and Sally went below to collect his papers and put them in his briefcase. A car was waiting for her and soon she was back at the 'glass house'. The first person she saw was Beryl.

'What happened?' Sally asked.

Beryl shrugged. 'No one seems to know, Sally. She was fine at breakfast, wasn't she? Remember how she and Johnny planned to look for shells this afternoon?' Beryl's face clouded for a moment. 'They sent for me at the school. Bob came down to see her and whisked her up there. I believe they had to give her oxygen.'

Sally caught her breath. 'And no one knows why?'

Beryl shook her head. 'They won't say. I think Gran knows more than she'll admit...' She stopped speaking abruptly and looked at the door behind Sally. Sally turned and Mrs Ester was standing there, gaunt, thin and angry.

'I suppose you've been enjoying yourself, Miss Hampton?' she said.

Sally caught her breath. Now what had she done to offend the old lady?

'It was very pleasant, thank you,' Sally said politely, telling herself not to blame Mrs Ester who was obviously frantically worried. 'I am sorry to hear about Mrs Dunn. Is there anything I can do? Should I go up...'

'Certainly not,' Mrs Ester seemed to explode, her eyes flashing. 'She won't want to see you...' she added, turned away and left the room, slamming the door after her.

Sally looked at Beryl and lifted her eyebrows. 'Now, what have I done?'

Beryl gave a funny smile. 'Goodness only knows. Gran's pretty difficult at the moment. Bob said a funny thing, Sally. He said this was a family that suffered generally

210

from "globus hystericus". What d'you think he could mean?'

Sally frowned. 'It sounds as if he thinks you're all hysterical but that's ridiculous. I mean, none of you are.'

'Doesn't hysterical mean giggling a lot or crying and screaming?' Beryl asked her as they walked upstairs towards their rooms.

'I think it means getting over-excited,' Sally said. 'And not being able to stop giggling. Bob must have been teasing— you're not a hysterical family in any way.'

'I wish...' Beryl said wistfully. She glanced at Sally. 'Paddy was telling me about last night. I'm so glad you got Johnny before Gran found out.'

Sally gave a wry little smile. 'I was terrified she would.'

'You rang Bob first?' Beryl asked. 'Why?'

Sally hesitated for a moment. 'To be honest, Beryl, I don't know why. I was frightened and that was my first reaction. Besides,' she added, although she knew that she had not thought of it at the time, 'Paddy isn't on the 'phone.'

'I wish I'd been here...' Beryl said.

Sally looked at her. 'You were out and I didn't know where you were.'

'I was at the Club. We're starting a dramatic group. Paddy found him?'

'It was Bob's idea and I told Paddy and he knew just where to go...'

211

'Beryl ... Beryl...' Johnny called from the hall anxiously.

Beryl gave Sally an unhappy smile. 'Someone must have told him,' she said and ran down the stairs.

Alone in her room, Sally went to the window. What could be wrong with Mrs Dunn, she thought. How triumphant Mrs Ester must be feeling, that is, if she was not too worried, for it looked as if she was right and the rest of them completely wrong. Maybe Mrs Dunn should have returned to normal living more slowly. Perhaps the excitement had been too much for her.

CHAPTER TWELVE

In the morning, Louella Dunn was definitely better, Bob decided as he stood by her bedside, but she was still a very sick woman.

He sat down, holding her hand, talking quietly, though she made no sign, except for an occasional flicker of eyelids, that she could hear him.

'Something has shocked you badly, Louella, hasn't it? That's the reason for your withdrawal. You've been hurt and you feel you've taken all you can. Louella, believe me, this isn't the way to solve your problems. They've got to be faced. Only by facing them, can you cure yourself.'

He waited but Louella lay very still, her cheeks had a little colour now, her body was more relaxed than it had been—but he knew it was like knocking his head against a brick wall—he was getting no farther. There must be another way...

He left the room and went to talk to Matron, an understanding woman, he thought, if ever there was one.

'I've got to get to the bottom of the reason for Mrs Dunn's reaction,' he said. 'I'll be gone an hour, Matron, but you won't be able to get in touch with me during that time. Think you can cope?'

The Matron, a sturdily-built, handsome woman with white hair, smiled. 'We'll do our best.'

Bob drove to the 'glass house,' ceremoniously rang the bell and a Polynesian maid answered it.

'Tell Miss Hampton she's wanted urgently,' he said. Then smiled. 'But don't tell her it's me.'

The girl giggled, dropped a sort of curtsey and vanished. Bob went to sit in the car, taking his time over lighting a cigarette.

The front door opened and Sally stood there. Even in the midst of his righteous anger with her, he thought how very pretty she looked. Her hair shone in the sunlight, hanging straight, it looked like silver. Her face was so clean, so free from make-up, her eyelashes were her own.

'I'm here, Sally...' he said sharply, leaning across to open the door of the car. 'Get in...'

She looked puzzled but obeyed him. Smoothing out her buttercup-yellow silk frock, she glanced at him. He drove away from the house, ignoring her enquiring glance, driving rapidly but carefully, lecturing himself, telling himself to keep calm, that he had no right to judge others.

'This isn't the way to the hospital...' Sally said, her voice suddenly scared.

'I am aware of that,' he said stiffly and thought how pompous he must sound. Well, he told himself angrily, he felt pompous, so what!

'Bob, where are we going?' Sally turned to him and asked.

He went on staring ahead. 'Somewhere where we can talk without being interrupted,' he said sternly.

'But ... but why?'

'You'll find out in due course,' he told her.

There was a pause. Now he was driving downhill on the circular road. He knew just where he was taking her—there was a neglected little garden with a derelict sort of Grecian temple in it. No one would look for them there—he could say all the things he wanted to say without fear of Sally getting

214

away from him, or someone disturbing them.

'How's Mrs Dunn?' Sally asked.

'Better,' he said curtly.

'She's not really, is she?' Sally said. 'I can tell by your voice.'

He looked at her for a moment. 'No, she isn't, really.'

'Bob, what do you want to talk to me about?'

'Mrs Dunn,' he said bluntly.

'Mrs Dunn? But why drive out here and...'

'You'll see.' His voice was grim.

After that, she sat in silence. He drove off the main road along a rutted grass track, through a tumble-down gateway and towards the cliff edge. He parked the car, turned off the engine, put the keys very obviously in his pocket and looked at her.

'There's shade over here and a bench. Get out,' he said. She was obviously puzzled by his behaviour but she obeyed. He waited until they were sitting down. They could see the sand and faint line of white where the waves came in. The coastline was clear, lined with palm trees.

'D'you know what's wrong with Mrs Dunn?' he asked.

'Beryl said you said something about hysteria.'

'Yes, "globus hystericus" but that isn't hysteria as you know it. The ordinary

215

hysteria means getting over-excited, being unable to stop giggling. This is quite different for the symptoms are beyond the control of the patient. Often she can appear calm and collected but the inner cause of the illness is emotional conflict which can cause paralysis or blindness. In this case, it has caused the inability to swallow,' Bob said, watching Sally's face as he spoke.

She looked puzzled. 'You mean Mrs Dunn can't swallow because of some ... some emotional conflict?'

'Exactly. But that is over-simplifying it. Louella's trouble stems from her childhood. Her over-anxious mother; a mother constantly making sacrifices for her and impressing on the child that she is doing so because she loves her. In addition Mrs Ester lost their eldest child and has always feared losing Louella. Her over-possessive protectiveness has sown the seeds of hysterical illness in Louella. She feels insecure and inadequate—to both her husband and her mother.'

'And she can't swallow?'

'No. Actually she wants to curl up and disappear. Life has suddenly become too difficult for her. Something has happened that has cut her last supporting rope.'

'I don't understand...'

Bob found his patience and calm vanishing. He caught Sally by the arms and

216

shook her.

'Don't bother to lie to me, Sally. It's your fault and you know it. You're in love with her husband...' he said angrily.

The shock on Sally's face was natural—or else she was the finest actress in the world.

'In love with Mr Dunn?' Sally gasped. 'Bob, let me go at once,' she said angrily. 'You must be out of your mind.'

He let her go. Then folded his arms and looked at her.

'Then explain why you let him kiss you last night,' he said.

She gasped and her hand flew to her lips, her eyes were wide open. 'But that wasn't a kiss, Bob. Not a real kiss...'

'It looked uncommonly like one to me,' he said gruffly.

She went red. 'You saw?'

'I certainly did. I drove down to see if you'd found Johnny and there you were, in Dunn's arms...'

Sally's cheeks were even more red. 'That's a lie,' she said indignantly. 'Mr Dunn was thanking me for finding Johnny and for not worrying his wife or her mother—and then he put his hands on my shoulders and kissed me. That wasn't a real kiss...'

Bob stared at her. Relief flooded him. 'Then you're not in love with him?'

'Of course I'm not,' Sally said crossly. 'Why, he's old ... well, not really an old man but an older man. He must be well over forty...'

Bob caught himself beginning to smile and quickly stopped. Had he forgotten that at twenty years of age, anyone over thirty was an older person? He shivered. Did she class him as an older man, he wondered. He looked up—the sun had suddenly vanished. A dark mantle seemed to be racing across the cloudless sky and even as he looked up, a few drops fell on to his upturned face.

He jumped up, grabbing Sally's arm. 'We'll have to run—there's an old building down there...'

They raced over the uneven ground, his hand on hers, but the tumble-down place was little security and at that moment, the skies seemed to open and the rain fell down—just a curtain of dense water that roared, splashing up from the dry ground, making them muddy, their feet sliding so that they nearly fell as they raced for the car.

Both were drenched and breathless by the time they got inside. It was impossible to drive so that they sat, staring at the windscreen that was completely blotted out by the torrential tropical rain.

When Sally could speak again, she turned to Bob, her eyes flashing. 'You mean to say you thought I'd be mean enough to have an affair with Mrs Dunn's husband?' she said indignantly.

Bob frowned. 'Frankly, Sally, I didn't. But the evidence seemed to point that way...'

'Evidence! What evidence?'

'Well...' He sought for the right words. 'The way you look at him. As if he is wonderful...'

'So he is—but that doesn't mean I love him,' Sally told him angrily. 'I respect and like him very much indeed. It's easy to see that you don't know the first thing about love, Bob, or you wouldn't be so stupid.'

'The kiss...' Bob said quickly. How little she knew, he thought. How he regretted those wasted days on the *Aurora*. She had been shy and much more naive in those days. She might even have grown to love him. What a fool he had been, he thought, worrying about a mythical adolescent dream of sailing round the world.

'As I said, when we came back I tucked Johnny up and left the room. Mr Dunn met me and was angry with me. Said I looked a mess and where had I been at that hour? Johnny came out of his room and told his father what had happened. We went into Johnny's room and put him to bed...' Sally spoke slowly and with over-elaborate patience, as if talking to a dumb child. 'Then Mr Dunn walked to my door and thanked me. He put his hands on my shoulders and kissed me very gently. Just as you would kiss a child...' Sally said.

219

Her cheeks were red again and for a moment, Bob wondered. Then he looked into her eyes and knew that she was not the kind of girl who would lie.

'Thank you, Sally,' he said sombrely. 'I apologize. Unfortunately, the trouble has been done...'

'What trouble?'

He heard the anxiety in her voice and told her the truth. 'I think Mrs Ester saw you.'

He watched the colour drain from her cheeks. 'Oh, no,' she whispered. 'She'd never understand.'

'No—but Mrs Dunn would,' Bob said thoughtfully.

Sally's hand was on her arm. 'Why need she know? It meant nothing—nothing at all.'

Bob looked at her. 'I think Mrs Ester told her...'

'Oh, no! She couldn't be so cruel...' Sally cried as if someone had hit her.

'She wouldn't see it as cruelty. I'm only guessing. I've no proof, no reasoning, just a hunch. Mrs Ester would see you as a potential enemy and would try to get rid of you. She probably suggested it was time you went back to England, and when Louella said she liked you and wanted you to stay Mrs Ester, desperately afraid you might destroy the marriage that means so much to Louella, would tell her what she saw...'

'But this is the best way to destroy that

marriage,' Sally said unhappily. 'Can't she see that? If Mrs Dunn doesn't trust me...'

'I think that's the basis of the trouble,' Bob said. The rain had stopped and the sun was blazing again. He switched on the wipers to clear the windscreen and looked at Sally. 'Louella would not be able to doubt her husband or you—but if she believes you, then she is virtually calling her mother a liar. Can you imagine the conflict that goes on in Louella's mind? Once again, her husband versus her mother. No wonder she couldn't take it and this is her way—unconsciously, remember—out.'

He revved the car gently, looking at his watch.

'Gosh, we must get going. I said I'd only be an hour.'

As the car squelched and skidded over the soppy ground, Sally twisted to look at him.

'What can I do, Bob? Shall I tell Mrs Ester the truth?'

'I doubt if she'd believe you.' He stepped on the gas as they got on to the hard road. 'Leave it to me, Sally.'

It was just as they were reaching the house, that Sally said softly: 'Bob, I'm sorry...'

He stopped by the front door and looked at her.

'There's nothing for you to be sorry about. I'm the one to apologize.' He leant across

221

her and opened the door. 'Try not to worry. I'll find a way,' he said.

He thought hard all the way back to the hospital and was then plunged into so much activity that he had no time to think until late that evening, when things had quietened down and he was in his room, with a book and a cup of coffee.

He lowered the book, turning his radiogram lower for he could not think and listen to music he liked at the same time.

What would be the best approach? How could he get through to Louella Dunn, he asked himself.

His opportunity was to come the next day.

CHAPTER THIRTEEN

That night, Sally waited until Vincent Dunn came back from the hospital. She was in the hall as he walked in, his face grave.

'How is she?' Sally asked anxiously.

He led the way to his study, poured himself a strong whisky and Sally a very mild one and told her to sit down.

'The doctor says she is better, more relaxed. Apparently they give her a drug called valerian which is a powerful sedative. He says she was absolutely strung up, her nerves at breaking point.'

He rested his head on his hands and Sally thought that he looked his age. A tired middle-aged man, desperately unhappy, frustratingly helpless.

'I know what it is,' Vincent Dunn went on and for a moment, Sally tensed. Had Bob told him what he believed had happened? But then she relaxed as Vincent Dunn continued:

'It's been the same every since we were married. I've been married before. Sally. A mistake of my youth,' he said, smiling ruefully. 'We had no children and parted as good friends but Mrs Ester has never been able to forget this and so she watches us the whole time, lest our marriage cracks up.'

He sighed, drank half his glass in one gulp. 'I don't know how much longer I can stand it, Sally.'

'Couldn't you tell Mrs Ester?' Sally suggested tentatively. 'I mean, in a nice way. That you feel husbands and wives should live alone and without interference.'

He smiled wearily. 'I wish it was as simple as that, Sally. I'm afraid it's something we've got to live with but I'm sure that's what's the matter with Louella. She tries to please us both and ends up by pleasing no one...'

Sally twisted her fingers together as she tried to rehearse silently what she wanted to say. 'When Mrs Dunn is better, would you mind if I go back to England?' Sally asked.

Vincent Dunn showed his surprise. 'I thought you were happy here. Sally, we'd miss you terribly.'

And I'll miss all of you, she told herself miserably. But since she had talked with Bob, she had made up her mind. Even if this little episode with them was straightened out, Mrs Ester would always be watching her, listening to what she said to Mr Dunn, reading things into innocent remarks.

It was a terrible thought and Sally had no desire to risk making Louella Dunn even more unhappy. So it was better, Sally had decided, if she left the island.

Another point that helped her make up her mind was Bob's attitude. Although he had apologized, it still hurt like the sharp twist of a knife to think he could have doubted her. What kind of girl did he think she was? It just showed what he thought of her, she told herself. It would be better to make a definite break—like the cut of a guillotine. Somehow, back in England she would put the pieces of her life together and start again.

She looked up and saw that Vincent Dunn was watching her thoughtfully. Would he believe her lame excuse, she wondered.

'Actually,' she said. 'I'm rather worried about my grandfather. He's very happy where he is but there's an unhappy note in his recent letters. I don't know how to explain but I think he'd be happier if I was nearer and could visit him…' It was a lie and she only hoped that Vincent Dunn would not know it. Her grandfather was happier than he had been for years and, with the regular arrival of her long letters, was certainly not missing her, Sally knew. But whatever happened, the Dunns must not know the truth—that the main reason was the fear lest Mrs Ester cause any more trouble, and Sally's own knowledge that in the end, it might be less painful to be thousands of miles away from Bob, when he could think such terrible things of her.

Vincent Dunn emptied his glass. 'I quite understand, Sally. But Louella's going to miss you very much. So will we all,' he added.

'I was thinking if perhaps it might be best not to say anything about it,' Sally went on. 'I mean, let's wait until Mrs Dunn is quite well. I'd hate to upset her…'

Vincent Dunn smiled. 'I know you would, Sally.' He stood up. 'All right, then. We won't talk about it until Louella is home again and quite well and then, I'll arrange for your passage. Perhaps you'd prefer to fly?'

'I don't know,' Sally said. Suddenly she wanted to cry. In a way, she had burned her boats. She didn't want to leave the island, or the Dunns or … or Bob. But it would be better this way, she told herself. Better for them all.

Bob was in Louella's private ward, standing by the window, gazing out at the slopes of the mountain covered with trees, bushes and tall palms. She had not reacted to anything he had said. She still could not swallow and had to be fed intravenously yet he was willing to stake his oath that physically there was nothing wrong with her.

He tried to imagine how it would feel if your mother, whom you loved and trusted, told you your husband was having an affair with a girl of Sally's age. First there'd be shock, anger with both of them, fear lest it was your age that had made your husband turn to a younger woman—then there would be disbelief. A feeling that you must trust your husband—that Sally was not that type of girl. So you would find it impossible to believe what you had been told. Immediately you'd have a shock—were you suggesting your mother was a liar, you'd ask yourself.

He heard the boy screaming and turned round, just in time to see Louella's body tauten, her hands clench. Her eyes were still closed and she was, to all intents and purposes, not 'with him', yet he had a feeling that she knew just what was happening. He drew up a chair between Louella and the window, sitting so that he was gazing out at the ocean. If she opened her eyes, she would

226

know that he was not looking at her.

He lit a cigarette slowly and then began to talk, in a casual way; almost as if he was thinking aloud and had no idea he had an audience.

'Little boys are queer cattle,' he said slowly. 'Take that youngster screaming now. It's only because he has to have an injection yet he's scared stiff ... It's a funny thing...' he went on. 'I've known tough Commando soldiers fight to the death with incredible courage yet two days later, keel over in a faint because they saw the needle.'

He laughed softly. 'That's odd, too. In Australia, they always call it the "needle". "I'm going to have a needle..." they'll say.' He chuckled quietly. 'I don't think it's good psychology—has a nasty frightening sound.'

'But boys can be as brave as anything over something. Like the boys at the school. They laugh at the boy from England who wears sneakers on the coral, yet these local boys are terrified of *tupapaus* which are a kind of ghost. Johnny's very interested in *tupapaus*,' he went on; by slightly turning his head, he could see Louella's reflection in the mirror. She had moved, had turned her head as if to hear better.

'That was a brave thing the kid did the other night,' Bob went on, still slowly, quietly and as if to himself. 'Paddy never thought he'd have the guts. Spending the

227

night in the jungle alone, like that...'

Louella's eyelids moved and then were still, Bob saw in the mirror.

'I can understand how scared she was when she found he wasn't in bed. She rang me at once...' Bob went on, carefully leaving out Sally's name in case it triggered off something. 'I couldn't help, I was up to my eyes in work here, but I thought Johnny might be doing something with tikis and whatnots, and sent her to Paddy Masters. They found Johnny—sitting in this old temple, proving to his pals that he was not "chicken"...' Bob said and chuckled. 'It was a good thing no one knew or there would have been trouble. Hysterics, tears, anger. But luckily she got him home without anyone knowing and then—' he paused.

Quietly he put a glass of water on the table close to Louella. Slowly, he lighted another cigarette.

'No wonder Johnny's father was grateful when he found them,' he went on carefully. 'Poor girl—he was so angry with her at being out late and then little Johnny came out and told him the whole story. That little boy has courage all right...'

In the mirror, he saw Louella's hand move and then lie still again.

'No wonder Johnny's father was so grateful. An ugly scene had been avoided, Johnny was safe and no one need suffer.

228

Johnny's father couldn't find words with which to thank her. I'm not surprised he kissed her.'

There was a sound from the bed and as Bob turned, he saw Louella's eyes were open. He understood the question in them.

'Yes, he did kiss her,' Bob said slowly and clearly. 'I saw them. I'd hurried down to find out if Johnny had been found. But it wasn't a loving kiss. It was just the kiss you'd give a child. For that is what she is. Just twenty years old and a few months. In her eyes, Johnny's father is an older man—to her, anyone over thirty is practically a has-been...' Bob chuckled softly. 'In any case, I happen to know for a fact that Sally is in love with Paddy Masters...'

He walked round the room, carefully avoiding looking at Louella. Gently he pushed the glass of water nearer her. Then sat down again.

This time he faced her. 'Louella,' he said. 'There comes a time in every one's life when you have to make your choice.' He paused. Her eyes were still open but she had not moved.

'Your mother...'

He paused again. 'She is destroying you, your marriage and herself. She needs psychiatric treatment but, as you know, would never admit it. She is the type of possessive, over-protective mother who can be a menace to her children. Fortunately you are different. You've taught your children to stand on their own feet. They love you—just as your husband does. He's been half out of his mind with worry about you...'

He saw her hand go out, touch the glass and close round it but he took no notice.

'If you leave Vincent, Louella, he'll go to pieces. You are his whole life. He only works so hard so that he can give you the security you need. Your mother doesn't need you. She has your father. Vincent has only got you. The children are too young.'

Louella had lifted the glass to her lips and was drinking. As she put the glass down, she spoke:

'But how could I tell my mother I don't want her to live with us?'

Bob controlled his face to hide his joy. It had worked!

'We'll find a way if you're agreeable...' he said.

'Bob, I couldn't believe that Vincent and Sally would...' she began and suddenly she was crying and sobbing. Great body-shaking sobs as the tears ran down her cheeks.

Bob held both her hands tightly, saying nothing, glad that the tension had snapped at last. It was a long time before the sobs subdued and the tears stopped. He gave her his hankie and smiled at her as she mopped up her face.

'We'll find a way, Louella,' he promised. 'This is something you'll never regret. Your marriage will be much more secure and happy, now.'

'But how...?' she asked, her voice uneven. 'Does ... does Vincent know?'

'About...?' Bob asked and Louella nodded. 'I don't think so. I told Sally not to talk to anyone about it.'

There was a flush on Louella's pale cheeks. 'She knows?'

'I told her I saw them and that I thought your mother did, also. She was terribly upset.'

'Poor Sally. How could I have doubted her?' Louella said.

Bob went to stand by the window. He, too, had doubted her. How angry Sally had been—and rightly so. She was not that kind of girl.

He turned round. 'Just relax, Louella, and leave everything to me. I'll keep you in here for a few days under observation and then you can go home.'

'And get up?' she said eagerly.

He smiled. 'And get up. Johnny's still waiting for that walk.'

She looked ashamed. 'I won't forget next time. Did he ... did he really plan to spend a night alone in the jungle?'

Bob nodded. 'Vincent will tell you all about it.' He glanced at his watch. 'See you

231

later.' He smiled at her. 'Stop worrying and leave everything to me,' he said.

She smiled. 'I will, Bob—oh, and thank you very much.'

CHAPTER FOURTEEN

Louella's recovery always seemed miraculous to Sally. The hospital telephoned the 'glass house' to say there was marked improvement, Mrs Dunn could now speak and swallow. The first day, only her husband was allowed to see her—to Mrs Ester's fury—but afterwards she was allowed all the visitors she liked, and on the third day came home.

She was like a new person, Sally thought. In some odd way, cleansed, her skin very clear, her eyes bright, her whole manner relaxed. She was very amenable to her mother, spent a lot of time with Johnny, but with Sally—well, it was hard to pin-point, Sally thought, but there was a difference.

Sally found it embarrassing in many ways. Louella Dunn was charming; friendly and even gay, but there was a reserve, there. Sometimes Sally wondered if still, deep down inside her, Louella believed that Sally had let Mr Dunn kiss her because he was in love with her or she with him. At other times, she felt that Louella was, somehow, trying to apologize yet it was something Sally felt she could not talk about, unless Louella mentioned it first.

Louella Dunn had taken her rightful place in her household since her return from hospital. Up early every morning to eat breakfast with the family, able to stay up late at night when they had parties. Nor did Mrs Ester protest any more, even though often Sally saw her purse her mouth with disapproval.

In the days that passed, Sally rarely saw Bob and never once alone, so she had no chance to ask him what he had said to Mrs Dunn that had so amazingly cured her. If her cure *was* due to that, and not to the drugs she had been given.

It came as a shock to Sally when Mrs Ester announced that she and her husband were leaving the island. She told them all at dinner, but obviously it had been well discussed with Mr and Mrs Dunn.

'Then you can come and visit us, Beryl,' Mrs Ester was saying, a slight flush in her sunken cheeks. 'In any case, your father says, in a year or so you will be leaving the island and coming back to England.' She glanced at her husband. 'I can't help feeling despite what the doctor says to the contrary,' she said stiffly, 'that this humidity is not doing George any good...'

George Ester looked up, his face red, and began to protest. Words that immediately turned into a choking cough. Mrs Ester sat back, her face triumphant.

'You do see what I mean, Vincent?' she said coldly. 'George had none of these attacks—not really bad ones—until we came out here.'

Later Rosalie told Sally that Mr Dunn had bought the Esters a very nice house on the Isle of Wight.

'It's a weight off everyone's mind,' Rosalie confided. 'Even when we're back in London, we'll have some warning before she descends on us. I wish I knew what made her decide to go back...'

'I've been wondering, too,' Sally admitted.

They were both down at the wharf as they spoke. It was one of the cold grey days that they sometimes had—the sky studded with threatening clouds, the ocean a menacing dull dark blue. The Dunns were going with the Esters to Papeete to see them on their ship, Sally and Rosalie were staying behind with Beryl and Johnny.

There was the usual fragrant scent drifting on the breeze, even the distant sound of music that despite the weather always persisted.

'Why had the old girl got her knife into you?' Rosalie asked with a smile. 'Did she suspect you and Vincent...?'

Startled, Sally felt her cheeks blaze as she looked at her companion. 'I...'

Rosalie lifted her hand. 'Don't tell me. I can guess. As I told you, I had the same trouble in the early days. Mrs Ester used to watch my every movement like a lynx. In any case, Vincent Dunn isn't my type...' she went on scornfully. 'He's smooth and charming but too much in love with his wife to look at anyone else.'

'Didn't you—mind?' Sally asked.

Rosalie looked at her and pulled off her thick-rimmed glasses, immediately looking much prettier.

'I like the job, Sally, so I took to wearing these glasses and very demure clothes and she soon forgot to watch me. I'm saving hard and in six months' time, I'm off to the U.S.A. for a long holiday. In any case, I thought it rather a scream for Mr Dunn, in all the years, has never once chased me round his desk...' she finished and giggled.

Sally turned and looked up at the high jagged mountain behind them. 'Are they really leaving here in a year or so?'

'Yes. There's nothing definite but I understand Vincent is selling his interest in the firm. He'll make a colossal profit. We'll probably get a good bonus. He's generous...'

They walked to Rosalie's car and drove back to the 'glass house'.

'You haven't been very happy here, have you?' Rosalie asked, taking a corner at speed, sliding a little on the sandy road.

Sally flushed. 'Very happy,' she said firmly.

Rosalie gave her a shrewd glance. 'The red-headed doctor?' she asked and chuckled at Sally's look of horror. 'Don't fash yourself, Sally, it doesn't stand out a mile, only I remembered how you were when you came off the ship and I put two and two together when Bob turned up. How come there's been no declaration of love?'

Sally swallowed. 'He didn't come back because of me,' she said.

Rosalie slammed on the brakes as they reached the 'glass house'. 'Then who was it? Louella?' She laughed at Sally's horrified look. 'Why not? She's a very beautiful woman. Who else?' Rosalie persisted.

'I . . . I don't know,' Sally lied. These days, she sometimes wondered why Bob had made no attempt to grow more friendly with Beryl. He treated her as he treated everyone else, politely and that was all.

'Bob has a thing about marriage,' Sally said. 'He's saving up to go round the world on a yacht and a wife would be a handicap.'

'I see. Have you noticed how much more friendly Paddy and Bob are these days?' Rosalie asked. 'They're always going out sailing when Bob can get a free hour or so.

They say he's one of the most conscientious doctors they've ever had at the hospital—always on call and cheerful about it, too. Of course, there's big competition, there.' she said with a laugh. 'The nurses swoon over him. I've often wondered how he stayed so immune.'

'He sees love as a trap...' Sally said stiffly.

Rosalie took off her glasses, folded them up and put them in a case. 'Boy, am I glad the old girl has gone. Now I can relax. Maybe love is a trap but I still think it's worth being caught...' she laughed. 'I'm dropping you off here, Sally, as I have a big date. One of the new geologists has managed to see me at last and we're going to explore the island this afternoon. You can cope?'

'Of course,' Sally said.

Inside the house, it seemed empty and still. She felt sorry for Mrs Ester—the old lady's eyes had been red-rimmed and she had kept glancing at her daughter as if she had so much she wanted to say yet knew she must not say it.

She wondered what had been said to make Mrs Ester decide to go back to England. Sally was sure that Mr Ester's health was a mere excuse. Sally wondered if she would ever know the truth.

CHAPTER FIFTEEN

The Esters had been gone three weeks when suddenly, one morning at breakfast, Vincent Dunn dropped a bombshell.

At least, that was how it seemed to Sally, although she quickly told herself she should have known that it was coming. After all, hadn't she herself told Mr Dunn that she would wait until Mrs Dunn was completely well before she left them?

It was a perfect morning, sky blue and cloudless, the distant roar of the surf in the background, the faint scent of tropical flowers drifting through the open windows. It had been so pleasant, Sally was thinking, since the Esters left. Mrs Dunn was like a woman reborn; much happier, full of energy, taking her share of the duties when they entertained, spending much more time with Johnny who tailed after her like her shadow. There were just the four of them for breakfast, for Johnny always ate earlier than they did so that he could be first at school, for he liked the chance to get Mr Masters to himself for five minutes, he said.

Mr and Mrs Dunn, Beryl and Sally were talking idly when suddenly Vincent Dunn looked across the oval table at Sally and smiled.

'I was telling my wife last night the sad news, Sally, but we both understand if you feel you must go back to England. There's a boat going next week or you could fly...'

Even as Sally caught her breath with dismay, for she had pushed the knowledge in the back of her mind as she hated it so much, though she knew that one day she would have to face it, Louella Dunn spoke gently:

'We'll hate to lose you, Sally, but if you feel you must go...'

'But Sally,' Beryl said quickly. 'I thought you loved it here as we do. Why go back to grey dingy miserable old England...'

Why, indeed, Sally was thinking unhappily, seeing in her mind the type of bed-sitting-room she would have to get in Earls Court or South Kensington, the battle to get to work, the battle home at night, the struggle to cook on a gas ring, the regular visits to her grandfather, who was perfectly happy without her. She knew that, from his cheerful letters.

'Sally's worried about her grandfather,' Vincent Dunn said. 'We can understand that.'

'Go by boat, Sally,' Beryl said at once. 'It'd be much more fun. You'd go via Australia and South Africa...'

'I ... I haven't really thought...' Sally stammered.

Mrs Dunn was looking at her strangely,

Sally realized with a moment of panic. Was it so obvious a lie, her desire to go back to her grandfather, she wondered. Surely Mrs Dunn was not thinking that Sally was in love with Mr Dunn—and that was the reason for her leaving them?

'There's no hurry, Sally,' Vincent Dunn said. 'But you did say that as soon as my wife was herself again and didn't need you...'

'I'll always need you, Sally,' Louella Dunn said and to Sally's dismay, her eyes were suddenly full of tears. 'But you must do what you think best...'

Beryl was on her feet. 'We'd better get going, Sally.' She glanced at her parents. 'It's a half-day at school, you know, and Paddy and Bob are meeting us. We're sailing over to the little island and having a picnic lunch...'

Sally had momentarily forgotten the unexpected invitation. It was Paddy's. He had rung up and asked both the girls, and had added casually that Bob was making up the fourth.

'Have fun,' Louella said.

As Sally and Beryl hurried up to their rooms to collect their swimsuits and organize the food for the picnic, Sally thought how different it would have been had Mrs Ester been there. She would have warned them about the scratches the coral gave that could prove so dangerous, ask if both Bob and

240

Paddy were good at handling boats, suggest they took life-jackets and goodness knows what. Yet all Mrs Ester's fussing was only the product of love, Sally told herself. It just showed how careful you have to be when you love someone...

The old familiar ache inside her was back again, the same desolation. Outside her bedroom, Beryl suddenly turned to look at Sally.

'Are you going because of Paddy?' she asked.

Sally was startled. 'Why because of Paddy?'

Beryl stared at her thoughtfully. 'Oh, Sally, don't pretend. You're in love with Paddy, aren't you? I thought he was in love with you but lately he doesn't seem to like any of us very much,' Beryl said.

'I'm not in love with Paddy...' Sally told her. 'What on earth made you think that?'

Beryl flicked back her hair, her eyes troubled. 'But Bob told Mum you were. He said he was sure that you loved Paddy...'

Sally's cheeks were bright with anger, her eyes flashing. 'Bob has no right...' she began indignantly. 'He's always imagining that I'm in love with someone or other...'

Her words skidded to a halt as she realized, dismayed, that she had nearly said too much. But her anger continued.

She stamped her foot on the floor. 'I'm

just fed up with Bob Chart. I wish he'd mind his own business. I don't go around imagining that every time he looks at a girl he's in love with her...'

'Hey...' Beryl got a word in, clutching Sally's arm. 'Don't bite my head off, Sally. I'm jolly glad you're not in love with Paddy. You see...'

It was Sally's turn to look surprised. 'You mean ... you and ... and Paddy? But I thought...' Once again, she bit off the words before she said too much.

'I don't think Paddy's interested in me,' Beryl confessed with a sigh. 'He just avoids or ignores me. I was surprised when he asked me along today...'

They went into Sally's room, both forgetting everything else as they curled up, Sally in an armchair, Beryl on the edge of the bed, kicking off her shoes, wriggling her toes.

'Oh, Sally, isn't love a funny thing?' Beryl said, studying her feet. 'As soon as I saw Paddy, I knew it. But he was always so strange, so ... so...'

'Impersonal?' Sally asked.

Beryl looked at her miserably. 'Yes, just as if I didn't exist.'

Sally was thinking how Beryl had changed since they came to the island. She had grown up, become much more attractive. Yet, Sally was thinking, she had been so sure that Beryl and Bob were...

'I thought it was you and Bob...' Sally heard herself saying and then wished she hadn't.

Beryl laughed. 'Bob! Don't you know his views on girls? He's told practically every girl on the island that he's not the marrying type.'

'He told me that the first time we talked alone,' Sally admitted. 'It's this dream of his of sailing round the world.'

'But he could take his wife along,' Beryl said.

Sally sighed. If only Bob loved her and it was as simple as that, she thought, what fun they could have sailing round the world together.

'He says it's no place for a woman,' Sally said.

Beryl jumped to her feet. 'He's never been in love, Sally, that's obvious,' she said and the words, that Sally agreed with, hurt. 'I'd better get my things together. See you...'

Alone, Sally began to look for her swimsuit and towelling coat. Of course, Beryl might be wrong, Sally told herself. Even if Beryl was not in love with Bob, Bob still might be in love with Beryl. Why else had he come back to the island, she asked herself. There must be a reason for it. He could probably have earned much more money in Sydney. He had planned to live there and start building his yacht with his friend—what had made him change his mind? Surely it could only be Bob's need to see Beryl again?

Suddenly Sally dropped everything and put her hands to her eyes. She was not the crying sort but in that moment, she longed to fling herself down on the bed and let the tears have their way. Everything was coming to an end—the dream that had never really been born. She would sail away next week on a ship crowded with happy holiday folk and she would leave her heart behind her. It sounded absurd, she told herself, but knew it was true. She would leave part of herself behind because unless she was near Bob, she was not really alive. It would be mere existence...

She went quickly to the wash-basin and washed her face and eyes in cold water. No one must be allowed to guess. Now she found herself wishing with all her heart that she had never handed in her notice. The Dunns would be leaving in a year or so, surely. Sally asked herself if it wouldn't have been more sensible to stay on that long and then leave them?

But it was too late, now. There could be no logical reason why she had changed her mind. Somehow, she would have to manage, Sally knew.

Bob was waiting impatiently at the wharf, the two sailing boats ready, when he saw Paddy's car coming down the road. For a moment, Bob thought there was only one girl with Paddy and his heart seemed to skip a beat. Then he saw a second head and relaxed. He had been surprised when Paddy asked him to this picnic and Bob had thought of getting out of it but had been amazed by the Matron's anger when he said so.

'Look...' she had said sternly. 'Your health's as important here as anything we have. You're working yourself too hard. It may be a corny idiom, but all work and no play ... It isn't a good idea, Doctor. You're getting your nerves tied up in knots. A few hours on the water, a little relaxation in the sunshine and you'll come back a new man.'

'All right,' Bob had said meekly, surprised at the strength of the older woman's anger. She was right, too, he told himself. He was driving himself too hard. He was not sure what he had expected to happen when he came to the island.

The advertisement he had seen in the Sydney newspaper had seemed almost like the finger of Fate. He tried to laugh at himself—talk about superstitious islanders, he had said. He had thrown away the paper in Sydney, determined to forget it. Yet the memory of it haunted him. He had found himself dreaming about the island with the strange spire of a mountain peak. There had been something strange about the whole business to him—why, out of all the islands in the world, had Mahane Island to be one that needed a doctor? And why, out of the newspapers he could have read in Sydney, had he to pick that one? In the end, he had given way to his first reaction. If this was the finger of Fate—gosh, he had thought at the time, how he would laugh at anyone if they talked this sort of drivel to him! Yet he knew the real reason. He wanted to see Sally, again. Let's face it, he had told himself. Basically it has nothing to do with the salary, the chance to save the money for your yacht, it is simply that you want to see Sally and here is your chance. You missed your first opportunity—you'd be a fool to turn down this second one.

So he had come to the island, not sure what he expected to find or do. And the first time he had seen Sally again, she had been hanging on to Paddy Masters' arm and laughing up at him, and then she had turned to smile at Vincent Dunn. She had looked so radiant and happy, that he had known the truth. Wasn't it obvious, he had asked himself. If Sally had been in love with him, even the slightest bit, how could she have looked so content?

Anyhow, Bob thought, kicking savagely at a tuft of grass for no rhyme or reason, all these months had passed and what had happened? He had been so sure she was in love with Vincent Dunn and Sally had been furious with him, saying that Vincent was an older man. Had that been a gentle—or not so gentle—hint that so was Bob? Paddy Masters was in his middle twenties, more of a contemporary. Why on earth had Paddy asked Beryl along, as well as himself, Bob wondered. What was the idea?

The car stopped and Paddy waved.

'Hope we're not late. You know what the girls are like—last minute prettying...'

'You were late...' Beryl began indignantly and stopped as she saw Paddy was grinning.

'Hullo, Bob,' Sally said. 'How did you manage to get time off?'

'Matron gives the orders at the hospital,' Bob said with a rather stiff smile. Was that a dig at him, he wondered. Had he been acting like a pompous smug creature, too hard worked to have time to enjoy life? He hadn't meant to do any such thing—but there was a lot of work at the hospital, and it had helped him endure the empty months by burying himself in work. Oddly enough, he had discovered that he was glad he was a doctor. He no longer wished vainly that he had been a sailor. Here on the island, where the responsibility rested heavily on him, he had found the sort of work he liked.

He smiled wryly as Paddy got organized and Bob found himself in the boat with Beryl.

'I've taken some pills, Bob,' Beryl said. 'So don't worry. I'll try not to disgrace myself this time.'

He grinned. 'Believe me, Beryl, you have my sympathy. When I began sailing, I was always sick. It's ghastly, isn't it...'

Beryl smiled. 'It certainly is...'

Bob was at the tiller, keeping one eye on Paddy and Sally in the other boat as its sails caught the wind and it sped past them.

'Paddy's soon picked up the art of sailing,' Bob said casually.

He was startled by Beryl's reply. 'Paddy's good at everything,' she said warmly. 'If only he'd realize it.'

Bob frowned. Beryl had grown up in the last months. She was very different from the meek, inwardly rebellious, teenager he had met on the ship out from England.

'He and Sally seem to get on well,' Bob said.

The sails caught the wind and the boat went scudding across the lagoon and Bob was busy for a few moments. Beryl was clinging to the side of the boat, her hair blown by the wind.

'They're good friends,' Beryl shouted above the roar of the sheets in the wind.

'Is that all...?' Bob shouted back, leaning with the boat as it heeled slightly. Somehow, he thought, it was easier to ask such questions in these circumstances. Why, he did not know, but it was.

Beryl put her hands to her mouth and shouted back. 'That's all. I thought...'

Bob nodded. 'So did I...' he bellowed and then shouted instructions to her to duck and his hands were full with the demands of the boat.

Sally felt the wind tearing through her hair, smacking her face, the spray stinging her cheeks. The prow cleaved through the swell of the water and she could see the small flying fish. She was filled with a strange excitement, a sort of exultation. As the boat sped along, she drew deep long breaths of air. This was fun ... she told herself. Really fun. No wonder Bob had his dream. No wonder he did not want to give it up.

Paddy said little, he was too concerned with the art of sailing, Sally realized. Normally he would have been teasing her and cracking jokes, but today he seemed quiet.

It did not take the two boats long to reach the small island. It was little more than an atoll growing up out of the reef round a tiny harbour. The boats sped through the wide opening, leaving the rough waves behind, slowing down as they hit the still water.

It was pleasant on the white sands. They spread a rug and Beryl undid the luncheon baskets. The housekeeper, Mrs Cameron, had done them well. Cool salad, cardboard

249

cartons of creamed tuna and peas, more cartons of frozen strawberries and cream. There were palm trees above them, moving gently, making patterns of shadows on the people below. Beryl, in a red bikini and a nose-shield, stretched her arms happily.

'How you can bear to leave this paradise, I don't know, Sally.'

Sally caught her breath. 'It won't be easy,' she said as lightly as she could.

Both Bob and Paddy looked up. Bob's red hair was sandy and standing up in little peaks. His eyes were wide with surprise.

'You're going away, Sally?' he gasped. Sally saw the strange look Bob gave Beryl—almost an accusing look, an angry look, she thought and then told herself she was imagining things.

'Yes,' Beryl went on. 'Back to dreary old England. She's worried about her grandfather.'

Bob leaned back on his hand, trying to relax. 'I thought he was perfectly happy.'

'He is but ... but I'm the only relation he has,' Sally said and thought how lame it sounded.

Bob stared at her. He was shocked at the dismay he felt. Why was she going, he wondered. Beryl had said Sally was not in love with Paddy but Sally must be. There could be no other reason for her leaving. Unless ... unless she was in love with

Vincent Dunn and had just realized it.

Paddy was frowning. 'We'll miss you, Sally,' he said.

'I'll miss you, too,' Sally said and, to her horror, heard her voice break.

She jumped to her feet and ran down to the water, doing a low dive into it and swimming towards the opening reef. The others raced down after her and all splashed and swam about.

It was Bob who broke it up. 'Time we started back...' he shouted, emerging with a splutter from an underwater dive.

Back on the beach, the sun dried their wet bodies.

'Your last sail...' Beryl said sadly, looking at Sally.

Sally managed a laugh. 'I'll probably take up sailing in England,' she said gaily. 'There must be lots of yachting clubs...'

'You like sailing?' Bob asked, sounding surprised.

Sally looked at him coldly. 'Any reason why I shouldn't?' she asked. 'Oh, I forgot, you think sailing is only for men.'

He went red. 'I never said that...'

Paddy turned to Beryl. 'Come on—you're my mate, this trip, and don't you dare be ill, or I'll join you...' He gave a grin and held out his hand. 'That's if you trust me...'

Beryl laughed, a suddenly happy sound. 'I'd trust you anywhere, Paddy...' she said.

251

She looked at Sally. 'Be an angel and pack the stuff before Paddy changes his mind.' She smiled at Paddy. 'Race you...'

Sally and Bob, temporarily silenced by the interruption, watched them race down to the boat. Paddy lifting Beryl in, laughing down at her.

Bob turned to look at Sally. 'Paddy's the reason you're going home, isn't he?'

Suddenly all the unhappiness and anger seemed to boil up inside Sally and she was shaking all over, her cheeks red.

'Paddy has nothing whatsoever to do with it,' she said angrily. 'Bob Chart, I'm sick to death of you constantly telling me I'm in love with this man or that man. If you weren't so darned blind...' Her voice broke and her hands flew to her face as she fought for composure. She lowered her hands and looked at him. He was staring at her with an odd expression.

'Bob—you know...' she cried accusingly. 'You've known all along, haven't you? That's why you're always trying to make me think I'm in love with someone else...' She went on, her voice rising with anger, 'You knew, didn't you ... From that time you kissed me, you've been scared stiff lest I trap you. Well, let me tell you this...' It was difficult to talk for she was crying as well. 'If you were the last man in the world I wouldn't marry you...'

'Darling...' Bob said and suddenly, his arms were round her. Tight. Warm. Holding her close. Holding her as if he would never let her go again. 'I didn't know. How could I know? You were the reason I came back to the island ... and when I got here, you were so happy and you had Paddy eating out of your hand and Vincent Dunn...'

Her tears stopped abruptly as she found his mouth so close to hers.

'Darling...' Bob said again. 'Didn't you know I came back because of you?'

Her legs felt deliciously weak. She was glad he was holding her so tightly as otherwise she might have fallen. She was glad for other reasons, she told herself. She felt slightly drunk—dazed with surprise and happiness, as she clung to him.

'I thought you were in love with Beryl...' Sally told him.

'Beryl?' Bob said. 'That child? Tell me, Sally why were you going back to England?'

If she moved her head a little, her cheek would brush his. She knew that. It was a wonderful sensation and very tempting but they must sort things out first, she told herself sternly.

'I ... I couldn't bear being so near you and thinking you didn't love me ... it hurt so much...' Sally whispered.

Bob's mouth brushed her cheek lightly. 'What fools we've been. What a fool I was ...

thinking a stupid adolescent dream was more important than loving you...'

'It's not a stupid adolescent dream...' Sally said indignantly. 'It's a wonderful dream...' She turned her head and found her mouth against his. She closed her eyes as he kissed her, let her whole body relax, as she let herself realize, slowly and deliciously, that the impossible had happened. Her dream had come true. Bob loved her.

She moved her face a little so that he stopped kissing her.

'Bob darling,' she said softly. 'Don't give up your dream. We must have our dreams. We'll work together and save and while you're away, I'll write you a letter every day...' she promised, holding him close. 'I'll miss you terribly but ... but I understand now. It would be the most wonderful thing to do. I only wish I could go...'

'You'd really like to sail round the world in a yacht?' Bob said, surprised, and then remembered George Soar's wife. She had said the same thing. 'Well, come with me ... It'd be much more fun with you,' Bob added.

'You mean it?' Sally cried. She hugged him and kissed him again and again. 'Oh, Bob darling, I do love you so...' she kept saying.

They were still planning their wonderful future as they gathered the lunch things, still planning as they got into the sailing boat, still planning as Bob gave Sally her first lesson in sailing, his arm firmly round her as he taught her how to use the tiller.

And, of course, there was an awful lot of kissing to do, too, so the return voyage to Mahane Island took quite a long time.

Not that anyone seemed to mind. Indeed, everyone seemed delighted. A double wedding, Louella planned happily. A contented doctor, Matron said cheerfully. A wonderful partnership was how Bob saw it, and no more loneliness. A dream come true, it was for Sally. Now she could live—where before she had existed. Happiness, she could now define for Bob. Happiness meant the joy of being together, of knowing you need never be apart again, the wonder of loving, of caring for someone, of being cherished.